T0006173

# subversive whispers

Celebrating 35 Years of
Penguin Random House India

# subversive whispers

## MANASI

*Translated by J Devika*

**PENGUIN**

An imprint of Penguin Random House

HAMISH HAMILTON

USA | Canada | UK | Ireland | Australia
New Zealand | India | South Africa | China

Hamish Hamilton is part of the Penguin Random House group of companies
whose addresses can be found at global.penguinrandomhouse.com

Published by Penguin Random House India Pvt. Ltd
4th Floor, Capital Tower 1, MG Road,
Gurugram 122 002, Haryana, India

Penguin
Random House
India

First published in Hamish Hamilton by Penguin Random House India 2023

ISBN 9780670096121

Typeset in Sabon by Manipal Technologies Limited, Manipal
Printed at Thomson Press India Ltd, New Delhi

www.penguin.co.in

MIX
Paper
FSC  FSC® C010615

*For P.A. Divakaran*

# Contents

# Translator's Note

Manasi is one of Malayalam's finest anti-patriarchal voices, reaching back to the 1960s. Her short stories have won her a very wide readership and her short story collections have won several literary prizes, including the prestigious Kerala Sahitya Akademi Award.

For the educated women of my generation who came of age in the early 1980s, Manasi's stories were early lessons on how to defy patriarchy—much before anyone of us had heard of feminism. However, sometimes, these early lessons are so closely absorbed that we fail to acknowledge their presence, their singularity; we forget what we absorbed into ourselves. I still remember the dizzy excitement with which we discussed, as college students, Manasi's explosive 'Sheelavathi'. The vertigo-inducing climax of the story, when we can no longer make out Whore from Virtuous Wife, was one of our earliest lessons in feminist thought that problematizes the Whore/Virtuous Wife binary. It was also one of our first exposures to the incisive feminist criticism of Brahmanical patriarchy. Manasi's 'Sheelavathi' lives in all times, and indeed, is the avid reader of the popular women's magazines of the 1980s, *Vanitha*, *Women's Era*, and so on—as she tells us in the story. We were chilled to our bones when, in 'Devi Mahathmyam', the narrator told us in cool, unruffled tones the price we were to pay for the place of Devi in Aarsha Bharatha: just your mind and your wings for sindoor and turmeric. But what always left me totally petrified while reading Manasi's stories was her masterful depiction of the unnerving violence that the patriarchal order sometimes makes its victims, women, capable of. There is something in it that shakes you—the power of patriarchy running through the woman, which always leaves her drained and disgusted. Violence that presents itself mutely, yet teeters at the brink of madness, like, for example, as manifested through the narrator of 'The Sword of the Princess':

> Seeing the golden sword lie orphaned amidst a thousand sundry things in the room, I felt insulted, like a queen slapped by a mere enemy soldier. My Prince up there must be seeing my defeat and humiliation. The sallow, wan neck right in front

excitement in Malayalam in the 1980s, we failed to evolve a broader conception of feminist literature that could include rebellious whispers and subversive laughter as well as the explosive, ironic, anti-patriarchal violence which did not however present itself as feminist in explicit terms. Feminist literary criticism of the 1980s and 1990s was extraordinarily naïve and short-sighted. It counted as 'feminist' only those writers who took the name 'feminist' as a descriptor of their writing, thinking and activism, and neglected others. This volume, I hope, will help remedy that short-sightedness in a small way at least.

Manasi's storytelling is a formidable challenge to any translator because of its subtlety—a quality that is characteristic of the literary generation of anti-patriarchal women literary writers who preceded full-blown, self-claimed feminism in Malayalam literature, including Madhavikkutty, Rajalakshmi and Ashitha (all of whom have been translated into English). She is without question one of the most powerful voices of this generation of the late 1970s and 1980s. Each of her peers had her own shade of subtlety (and Madhavikkutty, several shades of it), the forging of which was an aesthetic achievement in itself. Together, this generation articulated a 'female' modernism that expressed deep disillusionment with the promises of social reform and the Indian nation in the twentieth century—neither social reform nor nationalism liberated women from community and family and indeed, they allowed these structures to grow evermore confining for women. Unlike many black-and-white portrayals of patriarchy which came later under the feminist label (probably deserving the label 'feminist realism' similar to the more stunted versions of 'socialist realism'), the fiction of this generation of anti-patriarchal writers was sensitive to the ironies and dilemmas of existence under patriarchy, especially the pervasive pain of daily life and the sharp agony of breaking free. Manasi's writing stands at the cusp of rebellious anti-patriarchal whispers, sobs, even groans and grunts, and the unabashedly feminist challenges to patriarchal mainstream Malayalam literature. It contains the best articulations of both.

If Ashitha's stories feel like faint traces of pain etched inside oppressive, suffocating spaces, some of Manasi's best storytelling is surely in/about rebellious and subversive whispers, sometimes soft, sometimes rasping, but always echoing in the labyrinth of patriarchy. In such stories, it is the whisper-like quality that must be conveyed in translation. Some of these are whispers to the self—sometimes while alone, sometimes amidst the humdrum of everyday domestic life, or in the presence of a man, a husband or a lover. These men are also diverse—some are naïvely patriarchal; others, disgustingly dominating. In each of these stories, women from very different social settings speak—all of Manasi's stories are inevitably of or by women's voices that open up to the reader their inner worlds, struggling to capture the minutiae of their inner suffering. However, some of her stories do echo the triumphant and defiant breaking free, so typical of feminist literature. Thrumming with delectable (and terrifying) rage and madness as well as liberating violence, these stories are closer to feminist fiction than the work of her peers. But some of her other stories, equally feminist in their rebelliousness, are funny and ironic or even sad and strange; for example, the vertigo-inducing 'Sheelavathi' and 'The Sword of the Princess', and of course, the melancholic 'The Serpents of Tirumala'.

The worlds of Manasi's best work are mostly set in the 1970s and 1980s, but her writing continues to speak to us with urgency. Of course, one reason for this is that the Brahmanical patriarchy that she subjects to scorching critique is alive and well in our times, and expanding alarmingly, hydra-like. But it is also because the questions she raises are central to the ethics of the feminist life, relevant perhaps for all times. For example, in 'Square Shapes', she pushes ahead the question of merely escaping patriarchal power to ask about how one may find a place beyond it. And how one may learn to love beyond the social boxes that confine us as we continue to love those we leave behind.

I am so grateful that I was given the opportunity to translate Manasi; it is the only way I can atone for having devoured her feisty spirit and then failed to acknowledge its presence in my feminist self. Thank you, Manasi, for reading every draft and giving me your thoughts on each. My thanks are also due to all at Penguin, for their hard work and patience at every stage, and my first reader, Tomy Mathew. As usual, I remember my daughters, for whom feminism is the air they breathe. I pass on Manasi's superb and illuminating insights which my generation grew up on to my daughters and their generation of women. This translation is precisely the act of handing over to them this priceless legacy, of mothers and grandmothers.

J Devika

# The Serpents of Tirumala

Ammini Amma had sat down for her puja before the faded icon of Shivan on the ground, moist with the water from her puja jar and mellowed by the constant touch of tulsi and koovalam. On it rose the anthill like Shivan's locks, and she had indeed known that it would come this day or the next, and so she offered piously the water she held in her cupped palm, smiled tenderly and gently caressed the gold-wire-like snake that emerged from the anthill and entered her tresses.

'Your mischief! I have always asked just one thing of you. Do not give me another birth. Don't make things hard for my children. Uh, now drink this milk. Most probably because I have worshipped you and swept the grounds of the Brahmin home, the *mana*, in *eeran* clothes, sodden wet from a dip in the pond, the hip pain does not leave me for a moment. Let me see if the clothes left out have dried. Now, drink the milk.'

By the time she came back from the little open veranda changing the single-piece garment, the *torthu* that she had been wearing on her waist, the slithering one had left. Setting right the milk bowl which was now upside down, Ammini Amma pulled an upper-torthu off the clothesline and came out into the lane.

The morning was still chilly; Raman Nair sat on the narrow shop veranda as usual, still sleepy.

'On your way back from the temple?' he asked, smiling and lighting a beedi. 'The rest of us are only beginning our day.'

'No,' replied Ammini Amma. 'Just going there now. Am a little late today. The ladies in the mana—the *atthemmaar*—are going to be vexed. They too don't believe when I tell them that Shivan appears to me as a snake. I need a *nazhi* of rice, some camphor and some incense sticks. On credit, of course.'

'Thankamani's still at home?'

'Oh, I've dedicated my girl to Shivan a long time back . . . she can't be a menial at the mana. And I drove away my other child . . . before it was old enough to make sense of anything.'

'Let's not delay much.'

Raman Nair handed the packet of rice to her and went back in. It was Raman Nair who first received the information that Unnikkuttan was mowed down by a lorry. A chap who had gone to lift the *kavadi*-bow

2

on a vow to the Pazhani temple had told him. They say that Ammini Amma rained blows on Unnikkuttan who would not stop crying from hunger, telling him, 'Go to your old man for the money!' That was his father's eleventh death anniversary; Unnikkuttan left his home in secret that very night. Three months later, Ammini Amma received a letter and some money. She first paid for an ever-burning lamp for Shivan, then repaired the roof and framed a picture she had of Unnikkuttan posing with the Brahmin lord's children in the mana. When the women in the side-lanes saw Ammini Amma, they moved back reverentially closer to the fences and asked about him. And it was an Asari woman, Nani, who laid an offering of four annas before the anthills growing in Ammini Amma's yard.

It was then the letters and money from Unnikkuttan stopped coming.

She first said that maybe the mother of a girl, noticing his good nature, had fed him something to seduce him away from his own family. Eyeing Thankamani's luxuriant tresses and belly smooth as the skin of a banana tree, Raman Nair promised to inquire about him.

Only Krishnankutty, who used to graze cattle with Unnikkuttan stopped her one day, leaping off the back of the buffalo that he rode, snapping: 'Hey, go tell that

Shivan who you rear, who you feed gruel and fodder regularly, to make Unnikkuttan write a letter at least!'

'Oh yes, isn't Shivan a servant, mine and yours?' retorted Ammini Amma, smiling, untying and retying her hair, and rubbing her chest and neck, which were seared by the smoke from the burning torch of dried coconut fronds.

~

Ammini Amma sat gazing at the anthills, focusing on the spot just above them, in the dim light of falling dusk, beyond the tongue of flame in the ever-burning lamp, through the thronging smoke from the camphor and incense. When Unnikkuttan left home, the anthills were still small. 'Test me as you will,' she said. 'Ammini knows that moksha is not brought to one on a golden dish. Ammini is not one who gives up easily. But it is now fourteen months since Unnikkuttan left home. I am not growing any younger. It would have been really helpful to have him around. When I came up from the pond after my bath yesterday, Mathu *edathy* stopped me. "Devotion is all very well," she told me. "Is it enough for Thankamani to be just sweeping and washing dishes in somebody's house? She isn't a baby at the breast any more."'

Ammini Amma had not replied to Mathu edathy, she just hummed firmly.

She remembered Mathu edathy stopping her again when she had come up from the pond and was squeezing the water off her wet hair, 'Where are you running off to?' she had asked. 'It's only to you that she looks like a child. For the people around here, she's matured.'

'Why are people around here looking at her so intently . . .' Ammini Amma had snapped back. 'Is there such a shortage of young girls around here?'

'Well, I am not these young girls' father's sister. Thankamani is my Appu's child.'

'Oh! So, you remembered "Appu's child" only after twenty years or more after he died and left? Mathu edathy, I won't give her to you for your business. I have, long back, dedicated her to Shivan.'

'Pha!' she swore. 'Your God!' Mathu Amma ran up to the bathing ghat steps, the water dripping from her wet clothes. 'Where were these gods of yours when your boy, a mere stripling, was crushed and smashed under a lorry?'

Ammini Amma's gaze stayed on the swirls of smoke from the burning incense. The women who were standing around them caught hold of Mathu Amma and led her away. Nobody had told Ammini Amma about what the kavadi-people had revealed to Raman Nair. They were terrified of the snakes in the anthills growing in Ammini Amma's yard like Shivan's tangled locks, of their power. Stunned by Mathu Amma's revelation, the women desperately made vow after vow in their minds: because she was so busy with her labour in the mana, Ammini Amma had not noticed that after the news of Unnikkuttan's death reached local folk, Raman Nair had become easier with her payment for the puja items she bought, and that women had started bringing offerings to the anthills. A long time back, when her husband had died within two years of marriage after giving her two children, when she had wept fourteen whole days mourning him, the same thing had happened. Only when the senior lady of the mana sent their manager to her, reminding her that the mana premises were covered with dust and dry leaves since they remained unswept for two weeks, did she scramble up from where she lay in tears. She had been worshipping Shivan since much longer, from a former birth, actually. But her husband was annoyed by it and threw the idol into a dark corner inside the house; Shivan lay there immobile. And so, when the mana's manager came, Ammini Amma noted that she was all alone in the house, retrieved the idol, and set it right. She put the torn reed mat before the idol and laid Thankamani on it.

'Here is my daughter,' she said. 'Now it is as you wish; take or leave or do whatever you want.'

Then Ammini Amma stepped outside and shut the door. Entrusted Unnikkuttan to the carpenter Aasari Raman's mother. His wails grew steadily, slowly, distant. It was on that day she had sat like this, unmoving, before the anthills that would soon grow around Thankamani like protective armour. With nothing to say, nothing to beseech.

'This is fruitless,' she then said, looking at the swirls of incense smoke rising from the numerous facades of the anthills and their haze. 'You cannot but appear before me. If you indeed took Unnikkuttan, I am only happy. He was, after all, a good boy who didn't hurt a fly. If you have taken him, who will you take next? Thankamani has been dedicated to you since long. That leaves just me.'

Ammini Amma froze in her steps.

'Didn't you recognize me?'

'Oh, of course.'

Fixing her eyes on the bunch of peacock feathers on that forehead, Ammini Amma hurriedly pulled the upper-torthu towel off her shoulder.

'And so?'

'I am Shivan's subject. And not just that, I was thinking . . .'

'So what?'

'Won't that be shifting allegiance? If Shivan is angered . . .'

'What if I grant you moksha?'

'Ah, the old mischief hasn't disappeared from you,' she laughed while pulling a bunch of red and black kunni seeds from the creeper growing on the fence and giving it to Krishnan. 'How many times have you told the people of this world that you don't like mere worship and devotion and that you want good deeds done?'

'Hmm! Even after you see me right before your eyes . . . alright, tell me of one good deed you have done.'

That floored her. She couldn't recall a single of her good deeds. And therefore, nervous, she declared loudly as if discovering it then: 'Sweeping the mana.'

'Yes, I agree. That's one good deed,' said Krishnan, pinching the Kausthubham on his chest, 'but you know what it takes. Seven oceans, seven continents, seven mountains . . . it lies beyond all of these . . . to get past all of this, you need more than just sweeping a mana—'

'Alright,' she said, not letting him finish and taking some grains from the packet of rice she had got to prepare the sacred food, the *nivedyam*, for her puja. She offered it to the river on which Krishna stood, bowing low to him. 'Yes,' she continued, 'I don't want moksha, or anything at all. Just some news about Unnikkuttan. Where is he now?'

'Knowing beforehand what one can know is a person's strength,' a voice without a body rang suddenly from the heavens, like a clap of thunder. 'Keep waiting!'

Like she expected, Krishnan had disappeared. Far away in the distance, a single banyan leaf alone glittered on the river. Ammini Amma drew in her cupped palms some river water, as clear as tears, with a tender, loving smile, held Krishnan in her mind, and poured the water back into the river. She had thought that she would ask Shivan when he appeared as a snake before her. But maaya, that real-as-illusion, illusion-as-real from which the entire universe sprang up, would not permit her to do so. Stroking her emaciated belly, Ammini Amma walked on, ridden with guilt. She had not got through even a corner of a single one of the seven oceans. Seven whole oceans lay ahead . . . then seven continents . . . and mountains beyond. Deciding to start a number of fasts and vows, as usual, Ammini Amma did not tell anyone that she had met Krishnan by the riverside. When she told others about Shivan's footprints in the cow dung-smeared floor of her house, about how the anthills rose from the puja water-moistened ground of her puja room, and how the serpents slithered on her lap with no fear or hesitation as on Shivan's locks, they all had just laughed. Let all have eyes that are able to see, O Maheswara, she had then prayed in her heart. Why, even Thankamani started believing her only after Shivan roused her one night and led her out into the overflowing moonlight and the heady scent of *paala* blooms.

'Not fair,' complained Raman Nair, pouring the rice and camphor into Thankamani's waist-flap, ' . . . that you chose that Asari over some of us here, Thankamani.'

Thankamani lowered her eyes, holding still closer the tree-bark she had started wearing, which she had got from the nomads, the *pandaarams*' huts. Raman Nair, who had cast covetous eyes on the abundance of her thick flowing locks, which fell past her back almost reaching the ground, was suddenly blinded by the radiance of her hair ornament, which was like the fabled gem on the hood of serpents, and had to cover his eyes. The story of the loss of eyesight he suffered made the rounds in the village alongside the story of the illicit pregnancy. All the women there were terrified by the purity of Thankamani's (divine) wifely devotion. They retreated to the side paths and bylanes in her presence. Only the whores touched her tree-bark garments and feet and begged for her blessings.

No one was surprised that the child she gave birth to had three eyes (like Shivan!). When Thankamani writhed in labour pain, it was Aasari Raman who took her to the hospital. Only Ammini Amma expressed shame by pressing her finger on the nose, about relying on the doctor in the hospital to give birth to the son of Maheswara, one of the Trimurtis. Aasari Raman had been present, leaning on the elanjhi tree of the sacred serpent grove, too, on that fateful night when Shivan bid goodbye to Thankamani, and when she had stared at the many anthills there under the tree and wept, sounding like splitting bamboo; he had seen and imbibed it all. The sight of it had left Aasari Raman's old crone of a mother utterly alarmed, and throwing aside her bundle of firewood, she dragged him inside the house. Her worry was that his wedding, which was to take place on that very veranda ten days hence might be blighted by Shivan's anger. When he walked, with much remorse, at the head of the stretcher that carried Thankamani who was clutching her full belly and thrashing about in pain, his wife had tried her best to dissuade him. But she did not realize that he was following Thankamani despite that fact that his own wife had stood holding the wooden bars of the window of their house like a fiery coal because he remembered the task that Shivan had entrusted him at midnight in the sacred serpents' grove that moonlit night. Remembering the gem that had turned the shopkeeper Raman Nair nearly blind, he lifted up her

do anything properly at this old age. The lady asked if you could take over the sweeping, Thankamani. Don't we have to feed Third-Eyed a little something three times a day? Won't Paramashivan himself notice you standing by the window all day from up there?'

'Go and tell that no-good layabout of a father to feed him three times a day, you miserable hag!' Thankamani lashed out. 'Go find out who your Jadadhaari has eloped with now!' And she threw into the fire all the puja things that had been kept aside for the day of the vow. Ammini Amma tried to stop her, but the flame in the hearth leapt up. She had to lay down a sleeping Third-Eyed on the floor to go and sprinkle some water and rescue the incense.

'On which ocean are we now?' Third-Eyed would ask her when he lay beside her with his hand on her belly. 'If you cross the seven oceans, will you be able to see my uncle Unni maama, Ammamme?'

'No,' Ammini Amma would say. 'After that, there are seven continents. And then mountains.'

'So, you will have aged a lot when you get past it, Ammamma?'

'Um. And maybe I won't reach at all.'

'If so?'

'Don't know,' she would say. But Paramashivan won't let it happen. Even testing someone's virtue has its limits.

'Never have I neglected the *pradosha* vows and the fasts. Yes, I have asked Krishnan about Unnikkuttan, but I have made no other blunders, never strayed from the path of the snakes.' She would then hug Third-Eyed to her chest. Thankamani would not give him even a drop of water. Fixing her eyes constantly on Aasari Raman's wife, never moving an inch from the window, Thankamani wasted away like a rusting axe. Even when that woman went back to her parents' home for two months to give birth, Thankamani would not leave the spot.

It was on the day Aasari Raman came to know of this that he decided to leave for good. When Thankamani saw him bring Third-Eyed back from the hospital, she unleashed her rage: 'The miserable dolt of a man turned tail and ran seeing his accursed seed sprout . . . now go ask where the next seeding is!' Third-Eyed was walking up there, holding Ammini Amma's hand. Apparently, Thankamani shoved him out of the way. Not daring to catch the flash of the hair ornament, which struck Raman Nair nearly blind, Aasari Raman turned on his heels and ran without looking back. He entered his house and came down with a burning fever. And that was how he died, from seizures, on the morning he was supposed to leave that place. Not taking her eyes off Aasari Raman's grieving wife who was beating her breast and wailing,

Thankamani untied her hair, put it up again, took off her mundu, shook it well before wrapping it around her waist again, and washing her face well, looked at herself in the mirror.

'Add a mark on your forehead—that's auspicious,' said Mathu Amma, who was visiting. She spat out the betel leaves she had been chewing onto the yard and looked fixedly at Thankamani. 'Thankamani, truly, you don't look your age.'

Thankamani looked at her, without turning, in the mirror. Then dipped her finger into the ground sandal paste prepared for the puja and marked her forehead with it.

'Now redden your lips a bit, chew this.' Mathu Amma pushed the betel box towards Thankamani, not looking at Ammini Amma.

After Aasari Raman's death rituals were finally over, after the festivals of Vela and Talappoli were over, on one such morning in which the rain fell on the parched earth and rendered it mild and gentle, Thankamani had a stupendous change of heart. Leaving the anthills and snakes that were her protective armour and Third-Eyed behind, Thankamani lined her eyes with kohl, marked her forehead with sandal paste, went to Krishna Iyer's textile shop and asked for a gold-bordered mundu and an upper cloth. It was she who informed Iyer of her impending wedding with Shrikrishnan.

'If so, let Shrikrishnan give you the wedding clothes,' he said. 'Why trouble poor Krishna Iyer?'

Suddenly, the shop quivered like in an earthquake; people were stunned. Taking the new clothes that Krishna Iyer gave her along with many apologies, Thankamani told him he was to inform anyone desirous of seeing her in these clothes that they should come to the Krishna temple at Guruvayoor. Thankamani then disappeared like a flash of lightning in the sky.

As usual, Ammini Amma got the news of Thankamani's lightning-like disappearance from Raman Nair on her way back from work at the mana.

'It's all maaya, Raman Naire,' she said, leaning on the wall of the shop's veranda as she held the water he had given her. 'All those who stirred up my child's mind will also have to face the judgement of Lord Chitraguptan one day for sure, after they die, when they reach the abode of the God of Death! She almost hit me yesterday when I asked why the evening lamp had not been snuffed out at dusk. My heart had beat very hard then itself. But neither I nor my daughter has done any harm to these people here. Ah, maybe there's more suffering I have to bear. Maybe the evils of my past birth are still to be dealt with . . .'

Raman Nair did not raise his head. He only said that he had sent some rice and sugar with Third-Eyed.

It was that evening when she sat, as usual, gazing at the anthills and holding Third-Eyed close that she saw it. Inside the murky darkness of the anthill, a golden strand of light began to glow. Like she had imagined it. Ammini Amma ended her prayer abruptly. Not disrupting the divine slumber, not even moving the seat a bit, she got up slowly, leaning on Third-Eyed's shoulder.

'You didn't recite the prayer for Uncle,' he said. 'Um,' she agreed, not taking her eyes off that golden strand writhing there. She should not have asked the astrologer, the Brahmin lord of the mana, about Unnikkuttan. Maybe this was resented. That pose, with the hood lowered, was not a sign of a gentle disposition. A little knowledge is the cause of all sorrow, thought Ammini Amma with fear and remorse, folding her hands in prayer from where she stood. Not that she was unaware that the root of ignorance was sin. But when she saw the astrologer seated on the glinting floor with the *kavidi*-shells set there, she could not help herself. She had been very hungry, having gone without food for three whole days; her mind just did not stay at rest. It was all because she asked if she was fated to see Unnikkuttan once again. 'I will take another birth,' she told him. 'I will worship Shivan with a daily fast.'

'Ah, Ammini, you have still not escaped maaya,' said the astrologer.

The strand of gold seemed to suddenly twitch. Shining eyes from a risen hood stared at her.

Ammini Amma held Third-Eyed close.

'Your son,' she said, not taking her eyes off the hood, 'it's three days since he ate anything.'

The strand of gold rose like a feather from the anthill's hole and, shattering the anthill, it flew towards Ammini Amma. She could feel a coolness spread on her maaya-ridden external eyes, like a consolation. And after that, she could see everything. Standing on the peak of fulfilment, she watched Third-Eyed scream in terror, brimming over with affection for him. But things began to become difficult when it was evident that she could also see with utmost clarity all sorts of things: treasure-filled copper pots at the bottom of the pond, the yellow silk flying at the edges of the banyan tree, and so on. Things began to be affected, now that she could see so much. Even married couples felt that her eyesight stripped them naked; they avoided her. The worst affected were young couples in love, paramours and thieves. Because the large majority of people belonged to one of these categories, they, in general, struggled to keep away from her. That was why Dr Krishna Kumar, who had aborted the Brahmin girl Sukumari Antharjanam's illicit pregnancy, sent her away telling her that the medicine she needed was not available in the hospital. People watched the sight of Ammini

Amma holding Third-Eyed's hand and groaning and writhing from stomach pain on the hospital's veranda as though it were some intoxicating exorcism.

Apparently, when Krishna Kumar came near, she asked him, 'Kutty, is Sukumari better? It's been some time since I went to the mana to work . . . but the snakes tell me . . .'

Dr Krishna Kumar, who believed only in reason and science, looked straight into her eyes.

'I have barely four or five hours left, Kutty. I pushed it this far. Let this life leave the way it came. An abnormal death won't lead to moksha. I won't be able to meet Unnikkuttan again, if I die like that. Is there some way you could lessen this pain? Not that I don't know that one has to suffer what one is fated to . . . still, maaya . . .'

It was on the strength of those words that Dr Krishna Kumar initially decided to let Ammini Amma lie down on the pavement outside the nursing home at the dead of night. A life shared with snakes and peacock feathers was surely the whole *desham's* treasure. And not just that. Besides him, the police too were ignorant of the snakes' tongue. They were likely to mess up the nursing home trying to catch the snakes. That is how, in his effort to ensure her a peaceful death, Dr Krishna Kumar later sent her along with Third-Eyed out of the nursing home into the streets.

The next morning, Ammini Amma lay on the street side, sanctified and with single-minded devotion. The mild breeze blew some dust on her greyed head and face. It gleamed on her face like turmeric dust. The row of ants marching from the corners of her mouth had reached the ground. The crows waited silently on the banyan trees.

'Shouldn't we inform Thankamani?' asked Raman Nair as he separated Third-Eyed, who was sleeping with the suspenders of his knickers fallen off his shoulders, drooling from the corners of his mouth and holding a broken marble in his hand.

Since they all thought that the snakes would come, they said nothing.

The police arrived when the sun climbed up high. The crowd moved away till the measuring and noting were all done.

'Why do the *Naagams* need so much time,' Aasari Raman's mother grumbled. 'It's some three or four hours since the soul left.'

'Don't they have to come from Kailasam, Narayani?' asked Ammini Amma's sister-in-law, Mathu edathy.

'Know how far it is to come through the sky?'

The police hauled the corpse into the vehicle. People watched the sky with bated breath. They were sure that the *Naagangal* of Kailasam, the divine serpents, Shivan's companions, will not be able to bear this.

Suddenly, the *Naagangal* appeared in the sky like a carpet woven of strands of gold and studded with gems. The ends of their tails hung like tassels glinting in the sun. Though blinded by the radiance, the crowd could see, even though very dimly, Ammini Amma step out of that vehicle meant for unclaimed corpses and onto that golden carpet that the divine snakes made. They held Third-Eyed up and let out cries of wonder and joy; only he cried non-stop.

'Where did Ammamma go?' Third-Eyed asked Raman Nair, who squinted, sharpening his weak eyes, and watched the carpet of divine snakes fly swiftly towards the edges of the sky.

'Maybe to heaven,' he answered dreamily. Or maybe to Kailasam.

'Do you have to go even further from there to reach heaven?'

'Don't know,' Raman Nair said, not taking his eyes off the edges of the golden strands, wiping the tears that flowed from his nose with the edge of his mundu. He held him close. 'You have to go there to know. Come, Son. Nothing is revealed with these eyes so covered with maaya.'

('Thirumalayile Paambukal', 1998)

# Devi Mahathmyam: In Praise of the Goddess[*]

I am the wife of a very important official in this hallowed land of Aarsha Bharatha. This lucky woman, the owner of this spacious house, car, and every other luxury—there are times when I fall into such musings about myself. Sometimes I cannot help sitting for a long time gazing intently at my reflection on this large, smooth, shiny rosewood dinner table. When I sit in that chair and gaze at the world outside through my window, I often see poor women, their babies in bundles on their backs, walk across the top of the hill in the blazing sun carrying water in cheap and dented aluminium pots. That strange immobile expression on

---

[*] *Devi Mahathmyam* is a popular Hindu devotional text in Sanskrit that offers praise to the Divine Feminine, describing her—the Devi—as the destroyer of evil and sustenance of the Universe.

their faces . . . which cannot be scrubbed off or washed away, ever . . . it reminds me of stained, dirty small change. I am at a loss, often, about those. When I am about to throw them away, I inevitably think—it's money anyway, isn't it? And so, I put the thought back into my mind.

In our hallowed land, Aarsha Bharatha, women are revered. Amma said: Woman is Lakshmi, Saraswathi, and so on. And so, men adore us, calling us Devi—the name of the Goddess. And forget that we too are ravaged by hunger and thirst, like all mortals. What a pity, all could have been possibly Devis? The mistake is that we, all of us, continue to remain merely mortal human beings among people ready to make Goddesses of us.

Whenever I lie in bed listening to my husband's soft breathing, I remember Amma's words. Why did my husband choose me, when he had plenty of money and a golden future ahead of him? Like he says—a woman is but a burden; I know that too. I have learnt that from the forced smile that inevitably appeared on my father's face when he stood by watching anxiously every time some prospective bridegroom came to look me up—when I was made to stand apart so that my face, breasts, waist and other parts could be inspected and assessed. Once, on such an occasion when a bride-inspecting family walked away saying that the girl's fine but she's dark-skinned, Father flew into a rage, threw away the refreshments that had been served and strode off somewhere . . . His face, which turned all my heart's wishes into smouldering embers—it still wakens within me, sometimes. In such moments, I glance at my husband's face with a guilty smile. I, who haven't earned on my own even a single rupee to this day, have known well the value of money since childhood. The price we pay are our wings, our minds. I have always felt grateful to men who accept our clipped wings and our faded, soiled minds, to feed and clothe us in return. They are the ones who shroud us in pretty clothes and ornaments, smear the blood-red sindoor on our foreheads, hold us tightly in their hands, make us respectable enough to lug along. We are, of course, obliged to smile then. I can now agree that the clipped wings were just an unnecessary pretension. Gratitude, after all, is something women too need to have.

In truth, all complaints, even all requests, are excessive when you are worshipped as Devis at home for your large and wide-set eyes, shapely noses, and full breasts. What all does the world expect from men? That is why I am able to empathize with our friend Lalaji, a gold merchant, who has married a second and third time hoping for a male child. I, too, had attended his third wedding. Shaking my husband's hand with much happiness and pride, his mood changed and he ran his diamond ring-clad fingers through his greying hair sadly. 'Look,' he said, 'I am trying my luck for the third time. I only wish that God hears my prayer at least this time. I am getting old, Mr Nair. A home dominated by women is inauspicious.'

The mother of Lalaji's three grown daughters, his first wife who was standing behind him, held the hand of the new bride and brought her forward. Their eyes clashed on either side of the delicate fabric of her beautifully embroidered red veil. The bride's eyes were fixed on the smile that dawned on her older sister's face like the lowered flame of a soot-covered lantern. It looked as though she had suddenly sensed the real weight of the burden now placed on her. She never smiled after that. The second wife stood motionless among the dishes overflowing with sweetmeats; the keys to everything in that house firmly tied on her waist. When the guests left and the new bride, brought to produce a male child, followed Lalaji to the bridal chamber, the two older women were immersed in the ever-murky gloom of the kitchen. Their eyes glinted like pieces of flint in the dark. If they rubbed against each other even once, a fire would start and spread, I thought. I sat next to them, stacking away the paper plates and napkins. Lallu, the second wife, flung away the dishes in a rage, pulling open the kitchen drawers forcefully and banging them shut; she suddenly burst into tears. They flowed copiously, streaking her face. That day I stood quietly behind her, rubbing her quivering shoulder.

'Mother must already have arrived,' said the oldest wife angrily, getting up in a hurry and shutting the doors. 'Weeping on your husband's wedding day?' she rasped. 'What's wrong with you?' She started to say something more but stopped. Her lips shivered, like a small tongue of flame leaping up suddenly from searing, smouldering embers. Then, she looked at me. It was as though that flame was part of a smile like she was only completing a smile that had already begun to take shape. But that day she didn't complete even that smile.

I turned towards their faces which were etched now in my heart—as though it were branded with hot irons—and stayed there like inerasable scars on that day when I stepped out of Lalaji's house holding my husband's hand and thought: who would be our refuge if men didn't emerge and grow with their full prowess generation after generation? The girl who comes to work at my house, who carries her two-week-old infant on her back, Veena, even she knows this so well! That this was the price she had to pay for the health and well-being of her husband, who rested all day, pulling out the charpoy into the gentle morning sun and relaxing there with his hookah, and for the tiny hovel inside where she could sleep feeling secure. When you are expected to live all the time in guilt and fear, it's no surprise that you place great value on your protectors.

One day when she came to work, the child was missing.

'Where's your son?' I asked. Wide-open, parched eyes stared back at me. I saw the nipples of her breasts, swollen with stagnant milk, ooze and wet the soiled blouse she wore.

'My husband took him,' said Veena. 'He belongs to him, after all . . . We women do not even have our children . . . for ourselves . . .'

'But Memsaab,' she continued, 'he was feverish . . . tossing and turning . . . very uneasy . . . I sat outside the whole night hearing his cries. I thought I could beg for forgiveness when he came out to wash his face in the morning and go in . . . He, too, has a heart? Doesn't he know that the child will be thirsty? But no, nothing happened! Then, when he took the child and got out to go away, I wailed, beat my head, and ran after them. The baby lay limp, his eyes closed, not able to whimper even. I know, his throat must be dry. My husband was furious, probably hearing me cry and cry. The father of my child threatened to throw him in the ditch if I followed them! He may well do it—so easy it is for him to fly into a rage! "Please get him something to eat," I pleaded. "He is thirsty . . ." And I stood there, till they disappeared beyond the huts and the fence . . . and till now, rooted on the spot . . . Memsaab, why did God create women? Couldn't all his creations be male?'

Veena's sorrows flowed from her like a story. Then suddenly, very suddenly, she stopped as though she had seen God's face come up close. After some moments, she squatted in a corner of my large room and began to weep. Her blouse was stained with breast milk oozing from her nipples, her face streaked with tears—I saw them from where I sat, on my chair. They touched my sight first like gentle ripples, but soon they hit me hard like crashing waves.

'Veena, let me make you some tea?' I asked, having nothing else to ask.

Squeezing the milk out of her stone-hard, aching breasts into a tumbler, she refused it with a shake of her head.

Seeing it and feeling utterly despondent, I called to God, not knowing which god: 'Take away as many of our wings as you wish, but please return Veena's baby to her.'

God was always alien to me—today, every day. But because I didn't trust anyone around me to address my appeal and my tears, I called again and again to an unseen god.

Veena's tears and milk soon disappeared into the earth like water that had drunk iron. Bearing the burden of stagnant and dried-up breast milk and welling tears, she became ever-suffering like the very earth.

~

'The scriptures say *Kshamayaa dharithri*,' I told her one day.

'What, Memsaab?' she asked, smiling.

'The woman must be as patient as the earth,' I translated. 'Anger and lust and desire are all for men. We should be like Goddesses. Veena, men are born human and die human. We are born human, and we should die Goddesses.'

Veena was cleaning her big toe with the tip of the broom. She hummed.

'If only I could see him once,' she said. 'He must be walking now. He won't recognize me now. If I pick him up, he will scream.'

As I sat gazing at my reflection on the shiny surface of the rosewood table, I thought, yes, it is all true. Like my grandmother said, we should all be like the dutiful, chaste wife from our sacred Puranas, Sheelavathi. So devoted was she to her husband that in order to fulfil his desire, she would even carry him to a courtesan's house. Her devotion was undeterred by

29

his ill temper or the deadly diseases he suffered from! Sheelavathi, about whom our grandmothers reminded us constantly so that we could follow her ways. Our husbands' wishes should be our commands; if not, what will we do if they throw us into the street one fine morning? People will laugh in contempt as we stand there owning nothing but the garments on our bodies and the fading sindoor on our foreheads. Who will we beg for rice, in the teeming crowds under the sun blazing like the funeral pyre? If some god didn't spot my wifely devotion and grant me an *akshayapatra*—a cornucopia—or some such boon, I would be finished.

In the absence of these, it is better to have a regular place to beg.

Once again, I felt limitless respect and devotion towards my husband. When I stretched out my hands to accept this shelter and all these luxuries, I had nothing to give in return, except some love, clear and pure like tears. But that love was not something I could exchange. If I had to exchange love, the only thing I really had, that would have felled me. When I sit looking intently at the world outside my window, I will have nothing at all of my own. And besides, like my husband once said, even love is born of selfishness. I love so that I will be happy. Then what will I sell? The piled-up and ever-piling debts of my existence came at me like an all-enveloping monster of a wave, stifling my very breath. Three whole future lives would not suffice to clear them. If only my husband were not so rich, if only my sarees and my house weren't this expensive, my debts would have been bearable. Lost in thought, I saw that my debts were boundless, that they were ever-growing. Suddenly, like a bolt from the blue, I saw why they said that a woman needed to be forbearing. She needs to be grateful forever to her surroundings, even to her children. I felt deeply ashamed that I had to live this long to grasp even such elementary things.

This is how, though rather late in my life, I exchanged the proofs of humanity that I possessed—my mind and wings—for the turmeric and sindoor; those sacred offerings that I accepted with unblinking eyes and ever-steady lips. That is how I became, like all respectable women in the hallowed land of Aarsha Bharatha, a Goddess, a Devi.

('Devi Mahathmyam', 1978)

# The Far End of the Gravel Path

Once again, Santhi lifted her eyes towards the far end of the gravel path. It lay stretched out and sleeping under the heat pouring down from the sky.

Bits and pieces of the broken dishes hurled by her husband from the kitchen flew into the yard. Santhi was sitting under the moringa tree and scrubbing the pots. Her eyes lingered on the broken pieces for a few moments.

Then, as usual, she went back into the kitchen, walking right through the flying missiles and stepping over the fallen pieces.

Knowing well that he would hit her, she shielded herself, instinctively, with the freshly washed pots. The pots took the blows. He yelped in pain, rubbing his hands and stuffing them between his legs. The flat glass dish that she and Dakshayani had bought at the Vela festival in the temple was smashed. She looked at him again through its fragments.

Her husband was in agony, rubbing his hands hard. She could well pick up another pot and smash it on him now.

Why is it that I don't do it?

As she was picking up the broken pieces, he came near her again. His eyes blazed with anger. He stretched himself tall on the kitchen step and grabbed Santhi's exposed shoulder, moist with sweat. She dropped the pots and pressed her hands on the wall desperately, a slight scream escaping her lips.

He was going to bite her; she felt the hands that were holding her down scrape her breasts. Her husband's eyes were on her sweat-soaked cleavage. They crawled down to her firm waist.

Before his hands fell upon her waist to strip her, she said, 'Go inside. I'm coming.'

He didn't like that gentle expression of consent. His hands fell on her loosely tied up hair. Santhi slipped. The pots clanged as they scattered on the floor. Her knee hit the step. The loose end of her long hair escaped the man's clenched fist and fell over her shoulder.

'Ha!' he spat. 'Damn your okay!'

Because her head was bowed, Santhi could not see his face as he strode over the broken pots and dishes dragging her by the hair. Instead, she saw his worn toes with the ingrown toenails and his dirty, frayed feet.

She saw the thick, unsightly hair on his calves. And a part of his mundu folded up and tucked into his waist.

If she wanted, she could struggle, hit hard on that painful ingrown toenail, and the man's hand would surely fly off her hair. She could flee through the open north-side door to Kunhikkannamma's house. Pressing her hands on the painful bite marks behind her neck, Santhi wondered—why, then, am I not doing it?

Her husband had reached the door of the inner room. He shoved her inside and banged the door shut. The room was now filled with darkness. She touched once more the bite mark on her neck and the mundu on her waist which had come loose when he dragged her there.

She saw a sliver of light fall on his face through the door that had not bothered to close fully, like the shadow of a knife. The stubble, the pimples that protruded from it, the searing reek of perspiration . . . all of it stood revealed in that fading shard of light.

The pimples reminded her of the peanut seller at the movie-place where she had gone last week with her lover Velayudhan when her husband had been away in the forest to fell trees. He had thrown a pack of peanuts on her lap along with a coarse look. It hit Velayudhan's hand, which was pressed down on her thigh. Velayudhan's eyes, however, were wedged on the screen on which a woman was twirling fast, her legs increasingly exposed.

'Get the peanuts,' he said, not taking his eyes off the screen. 'They cost just eight annas.'

'No,' she said.

The movie tickets had cost all of the six rupees that she had.

'Good movie,' Velayudhan said. 'Should come again.'

When they stepped out into the dark, at midnight, after the movie, he caressed her hand.

She pulled it back, embarrassed. It was rough and lined with all the dishwashing, sweeping, and swabbing.

'It's as smooth as a fresh green leaf,' said he. 'And your belly, like the smooth shiny white banana stem . . . should come to see movies again.'

'Can you come to the house tomorrow morning, just for a little while? I had something . . .'

'When it is daylight?' he asked, 'Your man will finish me off in a single stroke!'

'He'll finish me first,' she reassured him, watching the fearful look on his face. 'You can use the time to run away.'

'Don't be scared,' she added slowly. 'I was just kidding. I can take care of myself, can't I?'

That day, Velayudhan slept peacefully on the veranda. She lay on her side beside him, staring at the open back door.

It was evening; she was just back from work and standing under the moringa tree. That's when Velayudhan first came to the fence and smiled at her.

She could still remember that moment when her mind began to bloom.

She would say, 'Let us go to the riverbank. It is really cool there.'

'What about your man?' he would ask.

'He's far-off. Gone to the forest to cut down trees.'

'He won't be back today?'

'Won't be back even tomorrow.'

Each time she waded across the river with Velayudhan in the fading dusk, she would tell herself, 'This is the last time.' But it felt good when the water splashed on her face forcefully. It felt good too when the wind touched the fine strands of her hair. How big this world is under the sky, she would notice. I can make my own path any time before I reach the far end of the gravel path, she would feel.

Velayudhan would speak just then. 'Run on and cross the river. I'll watch from here.'

In that lonely walk, she would kick aside the gravel. Why do I run like a madwoman to the riverbank at midnight, she would ask herself. These days, Velayudhan just sits on the riverbank. 'Go across the river, go on alone, I'll be lying down here,' he says these days. The packets of savouries he bought her from the tea shop by the riverbank—he would be fondling her, touching the drenched blouse all the time—she would fling the packets away forcefully across the fence as she walked off. When she turned to look, he'd be still standing there. In front of her, beyond the path smothered with darkness, lay the house. The door would creak when she pushed it open. She would go to the window and stand there for some time, gazing at the path. When she tried to push the night out and shut the door on it, it would resurface inside, on the gruel pot, and above the sleeping mat, gleaming like a floor freshly polished black. She would see with her own eyes the darkness fall in shards like ripples on the river. It was when they grew in a heap under her feet that she felt the fear. She had often heard the night stack up the darkness in layers when she lay on the mat, covering herself from top to toe but with eyes wide open.

Her husband was tired now. When he grabbed her hair, it had ached right down to somewhere below the skin and the bone.

He had begun to fall asleep. Removing his hand from her body, Santhi rose from the mat and stood up straight. She wiped her face and belly hard with the edge of her mundu. He lay there asleep, flat on his back with his mouth open and legs apart. She stood still for a few moments, looking at him. He was to leave tomorrow for the forest and would be back only weeks later. Velayudhan would come tomorrow night. He would knock gently on the window. The coolness of the riverbank came back into her memory. When she opened the window, he would ask, 'Your man won't be back tomorrow?'

Standing on this side of the window, she would knock about that question in her mind: should I go? Or shouldn't I?

'Your boobs are now bigger than before!'

'Ah! Magic, it is!'

'Make them bigger!'

'My man doesn't like that.'

Velayudhan would fall silent then.

Her husband turned in his sleep, and his flung-apart leg came under her foot. Santhi stared at his feet for some time. Dirty, lined feet.

She casually took out the large machete from under the pillow. The pillow moved a little. But the man didn't wake up. Santhi stood there looking at her husband in the light that splattered around the room through the door which was open just a crack. He still lay sleeping, head on one side, legs flung apart, hands open on the floor, mouth open and drooling.

Motionless for some moments, Santhi then gently shook him.

She brandished the machete so that he could see it clearly.

I don't need the ignominy of murdering a sleeping man. And besides, when they met at the riverbank, if Velayudhan asked her if she wasn't adept at setting traps, she would have no answer even.

Santhi kicked him this time to wake him up. He woke and scrambled up angrily, and since the sight of Santhi brandishing a machete was totally unexpected, he let out an ugly sound of fear. His stupor drained off instantly.

'What's your name?'

'Dinakaran.'

'No. Velayudhan.'

'Velayudhan.' He repeated after her obediently.

'Who's Velayudhan?' Santhi asked.

'I don't know.'

Santhi was quite amused to see him petrified by the sight of her wielding the machete.

She gripped it even more tightly.

'I want to go to the riverbank,' she said. The Vela festival was on. She wanted to go to the fair.

'This very afternoon?'

'Yes.'

'I'll take you there.'

39

'There's plenty of water in the river. You'll carry me.'
'I know.'
'You'll get me glass bangles and anklets from the fair.'
'Yes, I will.'

But suddenly she thought: it is not any of these that I really want. The bangles that Velayudhan bought her were still unworn. The anklets, too.

So, she said, 'All that can wait. For now, wipe my feet with your mundu.'

He bent down.

He'll notice that my toenails are beginning to be ingrown and that the heels and balls of my feet are dry and cracked, she remembered anxiously. The same disgust that she had felt at the sight of his feet must be bubbling in his mind as well.

She felt the hatred fall like flakes off a scab in her mind. Her husband was still crouching at her feet, waiting for permission to rise.

'Around this room on your knees three times,' she ordered, avoiding his face.

She said that and immediately thought: why did I demand that? It made her wonder . . .

~

That machete had always been there under the pillow—close enough for her to pull it out any time.

I can tell him to throw open this door now if I want, thought Santhi, looking at her husband dragging himself around the room on his knees, and gripping the weapon hard. I can hold this and stride on the gravel path to its farthest end, cross the river, and go beyond. I can tie up this husband on a stump like a guard dog.

But she would never do any of this.

Like trying to regain balance on an invisible tightrope, she gripped the machete even more tightly. Where did I falter, she had asked herself many times. I don't know where the strings are. If I mention this machete to Velayudhan, he will only stare at me stunned as though I had given him a tight slap.

And after, while at the movies, he'll probably check in the dark if I am holding a machete.

I might forget to laugh when we sit on the cool sand by the river.

The husband had finished circling the room three times on his knees and was at her feet now.

Her husband's thick, naked, sweaty neck below her, between her feet.

Outside, Velayudhan's stupefied face has forgotten how to smile.

If this machete slipped just a little bit, how forcefully would he knock me down—Santhi tried to think. Once that was done, he would wipe hard the sweat on his neck and lock the door from the outside like before.

She would wait for the night and strain her ears for the sound of the duplicate key that Velayudhan would bring.

Santhi felt disgust spewing forth in her mind like the pus breaking out of a malignant sore. It was when its stink became unbearable that she swung the machete towards her head, like a sob long suppressed that escaped, nevertheless. She saw for a moment the red splatter on the face of her husband, who crouched below seeking permission to get up. And then it disappeared into a torrent of indescribable relief.

('Charalpathayude Dooram', 1994)

# The Walls

My house had walls that were so thick, no one outside could have any inkling of what went on inside. My Ammavan, senior maternal uncle and the head of our *taravad*, was a powerful landlord. He had his photo framed and mounted on the wall of the portico of the house; on its side was an equally large-framed image of Mahatma Gandhi. Ammavan had big hands; his forehead was always marked with several streaks of sacred ash. All of us stood before him with our bodies bowed in extreme respect—upper cloths tied around our waists, faces and torsos bent towards the ground, hands covering mouths. Only the white doves paid no attention to him. They fluttered about in the open space in front of the portico and cooed aloud. That's probably why he used to shoot them from the portico sometimes. But I was very fond of them. Because he never had to work, Ammavan's hands were very soft and smooth. The locals declared before him that his mind was as tender. They told me the same too.

When the day drew to an end, Ammavan would summon all the children of the family. Stretching out on the big easy chair made of rosewood, rubbing his expansive forehead, he would tell us: 'Be diligent in your studies. Never tell a lie. Only good people are born in our taravad.'

I once picked and ate a tender cucumber in stealth from the garden outside our house. I had fooled my mother and my ayah. I did it with Paramu ettan, my brother. The next morning, I woke up rudely hearing the screams of Chelli, the *cheruman*, who used to graze our cattle. He was tied to the tall pillar on our veranda. Ammavan sat on a high stool holding a cup of tea in one hand and a whip in the other. The cheruman shuddered at every lash. The lash marks grew cold on his body. From behind the blue curtains, behind the railings of the window above, I watched Chelli being beaten for a long time—beaten because I didn't tell the truth about stealing the tender cucumber. A shard of sunlight that was beginning to grow stronger had fallen on Chelli's withered cheek. His eyes were so parched that they looked incapable of ever shedding another tear.

That evening when we children were summoned before him, Ammavan said, 'If you lie and steal, then people will beat you just like I beat Chelli cheruman this morning.' I exchanged a glance with Paramu ettan. A smile glinted in ettan's eyes. I suddenly remembered Chelli's parched eyes. Of course, I wasn't grown up then, I was merely a child. A time in which the white doves and Chelli's eyes looked beautiful. So, I spoke up, 'Ammava, it was I who stole the tender cucumber.'

Ammavan was suddenly annoyed. 'Did someone ask you? I beat Chelli so that he won't steal ever.'

The manager of our taravad, Ramu Nair, was easily given to a foul temper. His unmarried niece got pregnant. One night, he pushed Lakshmikkutty against a wall and kicked her hard. The whole world soon knew that he had quietly buried her corpse at midnight. But Ammavan laughed as he chewed pieces of fried meat: 'Ramu naire, not a hair on your body will be harmed as long as I am here. Tell that Sankara Menon who's in the police, to come down. This taravad has never abandoned its dependents.'

The day Sankara Menon visited, Ammavan shot a rabbit. When Sankara Menon left after a hearty meal and generous betel-chewing, he had a smile on his face—of a sort that I could never forget. I have seen many such smiles since.

That's why I asked Ramu Nair, when we were on our way to the temple in the covered bullock cart, about how Lakshmikkutty had died. His face turned wrathful for a moment.

'Let that be,' he said, 'why is My Lady thinking about such things?'

'Did you kick her to death?'

'Hey, no! She was bitten by a snake . . . the poison spreads fast after dusk. Your Ammavan knows all about it, Ammu. It was a big serpent! Your Ammavan knows.' I was around twenty then. Around then I had begun to read novels from the village library. I gazed at his face intently—like in those novels. But he said, 'Your Ammavan is God in these parts!' He wiped off the betel-stained saliva and leaned on one side inside the cart.

'Does Chelli cheruman say the same?' I asked.

It was years since Chelli cheruman died. Ammavan made sure that his sixteenth-day death ceremony was quite grand.

'He's taken many blows from me,' he said. 'The sixteenth-day feast must be splendid.'

I was in love with Chelli's handsome son, Chami.

'Chami,' I would tell him, 'If you call me to you, O Lord of my heart, I will follow you to the end of the earth.'

I had obtained this sentence, too, from the novels that I read greedily.

One day, Ammavan caught us together in the large barn in our house.

Chami and Ammavan held each other's gaze for a long time. Ammavan never looked at my face. He snorted decisively and walked off—and Chami called me, 'Come, let us go to the end of the earth!'

But I didn't move. Chami pulled off the towel on his shoulder, shook it noisily, and tied it on his head before he stepped out to leave.

Then, steeped in the memory of Chami's blazing eyes, I married the son of the landlord from the neighbouring village. Chami was taken away, right before my eyes, from our usual meeting place; it was Ramu Nair who took him. I could have committed suicide in protest, like in the novels. But my bridegroom was handsome too, like Chami. And anyway, by then, Chami was dead.

The day before my wedding, I took Ammavan's *kora* porridge to him. He was reading the Bhagavad Geetha. Handing him the porridge, I asked, 'How was Chami killed?'

'Beaten to death,' he said, 'Uh?'

'Nothing. Just wanted to see if you lie, Ammava.'

He lifted the edge of his *khaddar* mundu, wiped his chin, and gave me the empty glass. One fine morning when the Grama Sevaks got busy uplifting our villages, Ammavan began to rear fowl within the heavy soundproof outer walls of our house. That's how Progress arrived in our front yard. In public meetings,

Ammavan spoke tirelessly and regularly for the poor. In some pallid afternoons, when there were no meetings, he strangled to death some of the fowls that lay tired and broken inside the big nets in the yard. He ate them at night. Also, it was Ammavan who secured a library for our village.

Not just my younger aunt's son Raghu but also the Christian Anthoni—and Gopi, who had called Ammavan a reactionary old geezer at the meeting at Ambalakkunnu—sat on the veranda. Along with Raghu. I watched—through the wooden railings of the north-side window—Ammavan pace inside the courtyard between the four wings of our inner rooms with a low snarl under his breath all the while. My younger aunt would be in a corner of the north-side room, wiping her eyes and nose with the edge of her upper cloth.

'Ammava,' Raghu said. 'Mohanan doctor has certified that Paalan cheruman died not of Sankara Menon's blows but because of a snake bite. Raman Nair has the certificate.'

When Raghu turned to step in, Ammavan stopped him. 'Stop there, *eda*.'

'What for?' He sounded very calm. 'I need to take a nap.'

Maybe because his eyes fell on Raghu's face, Ammavan went off quickly towards the veranda.

Raghu's guffaw that made the roof shake followed. My younger aunt's sobs grew stronger. Because the number of people dying of snakebites seemed to be growing in our village.

Listening to the sound of Raghu climbing the steps, my mother said, 'Serves Paalan, right! The blasphemy he was spewing!'

Just days before, Paalan had stood in the open space in front of our portico facing Ammavan. His mundu was hitched up on his waist brashly; a lit bidi smouldered on his lips. His lips quivered in a rage as he spoke. The hair above his lips was barely dark. His face overflowed with the zest and truth that is so common at his age.

It was through the north-side window that I observed Paalan's face. His fury made me laugh. There's just one thing that we lose as we grow older— the ruddiness and the life that were visible on Paalan's face, precisely.

Paalan was the only cheruman to have passed the matriculation exam in our village. 'So, we must make his sixteenth-day death feast absolutely impressive,' said Ammavan. He ran about organizing a magnificent feast, and Paalan's old crone of a mother fell at Ammavan's feet and wept copiously. 'Lord,' she cried, 'Tambra . . . you are a big man. God will bless you!' Her tears that wheezed like the rain were met with the

49

lightning and thunder of the laughter that flashed on Ammavan's face. It has burned and seared the wings of all the white doves that were to fly into my courtyard, I felt.

Keeping that smile alive on his face, Ammavan told the children of the house: 'Grown-ups are your gurus. The worst sin is to insult one's guru. What else do we older folk think of, children, except your well-being?'

Ammavan listened silently to Raghu's explosive laugh. Then, with a faint smile glimmering on his lips, he lifted my little daughter onto his lap. His face was like a gravelly yard that never saw a hoe.

I remembered all this today because Paalan's mother brought a large gourd from her garden as a serf's gift for Ammavan's sixtieth birthday celebration. 'My Lady,' she said. 'If Paalan was alive, he'd have brought a big bunch of bananas!'

I stared at her greyed head and weak eyes for some time and asked, 'How long is it since he died?'

'Fourteen years,' said Kurumba, 'Why do you ask, My Lady?'

'Nothing in particular,' I said. 'Won't you have lunch before you go?'

As I stepped into the vestibule, Raghu, who came opposite me, stopped suddenly.

'*Oppole,*' he addressed me as his sister, 'tell Velu to take the white gourd Kurumba brought to the kitchen.

Also, tell him to give the hag a mundu. That's our Paalan's old woman.'

Raghu's temples had begun to grey. His khaddar shirt was flecked with betel stains. The colour of dried blood. He was grown now. I thought, if he drew himself up to his full height, his head would touch the top of the door of the portico.

'Why are you standing there rooted, oppole?' He asked, turning, as he got into the darkness of the four wings of rooms from the vestibule, 'Velu is at the veranda of the barn.'

'Raghu, Ammavan usually gives Paalan's old mum two pieces of mundukal,' I reminded him. 'You can do that too, can't you?'

('Mathilukal', 1975)

# Square Shapes

Saraswathi found a lover utterly by chance. That reality wrapped itself around her; it was like a circle, the origin and end of which were not distinguishable. In the beginning, it left her quite breathless. Her lover's face would flash through her mind like a streak of lightning throughout the day—while asking her husband what curry he'd like for lunch, while playing with her little son on her lap, while bursting into tears in the shower amid the abundance of sparkling drops of water for no particular reason. Much of what her mind had gathered as unassailable truth was suddenly losing all meaning, she would feel. Her mind would quiver then as though it were pivoted on her finger.

'Free-flowing romance?' she asked herself as she sat gazing at the pretty gold bangles her husband bought her, 'why are minds like this?'

'So, how are minds to be?' Seetha would ask. 'Like coffee with a lid on top so that flies won't fall into it? Gone cold and with a repulsive skin on the top?'

From the day of this conversation, these questions stayed in Saraswathi's mind. Sometimes, Seetha's face which had flushed as she asked them would serve as an answer. Seetha's face was the rosy red of early dawn. The truth and justice of it are all in that ruddy hue, Saraswathi would say.

And then, in time, the lover became familiar to her, like a frequent dream, like a face seen every day on the street.

Saraswathi continued to sew buttons on her husband's shirts and wash her child's milk bottle carefully. The fragrance of the forest of chempaka blooms that had grown wild in a corner of her mind enveloped her and her home. Bearing that alluring scent in her body and space, she cooked for her husband. Cleaned the house. Fed the child. Made her husband laugh.

Once, after the lover had visited and left, when she lay in her husband's arms with a limpid smile, Saraswathi asked, 'Tell me, what is this thing called morality?'

Her husband tightened his arms around her and said, 'Here, it is this.'

'Suppose I had a lover . . .' Saraswathi began.

'Then I will kill him today,' her husband laughed.

'And then?' she asked. 'I will still love him. Maybe even more.'

'Then,' her husband said. 'I will kill you too.'

'And then?' she persisted.

When silence began to form a pool, she reassured him: 'Sleep. I was just joking.'

What is the hurry to enclose everything within square shapes? No one can tuck everything snugly, nicely, prettily into square shapes.

That's how Saraswathi asked her lover about the colour of happiness when they were sitting beside a frothy, playful sea.

'The colour of your face,' Raghu told her.

Then maybe, here, it is the colour of the sea. Maybe the colour of the sky, of dreams, of everything open.

'Look, Raghu,' she said, 'I think now I can hold the world in my cupped hands.'

'When was it impossible?' Raghu asked.

'We, each of us, exceed all square shapes. But we stay within them. Come out, take courage, and see—and you'll want to laugh and weep at the same time for those who you left behind. You'll want to hug them close, give them love. We can be seas then or skies. We can be all of us.'

Returning to her husband always felt like climbing down from the sky into a clam. As she lay beside her husband feeling fresh after a bath and running her fingers through her long open hair, she remembered the little ripples playing on the sand banks. She yearned to fall asleep to their music, feeling the soft, pleasurable touch of the cool, endearing little waves. She felt herself to be the silent, smiling, serene meadow of grass beneath a gentle breeze.

A sense of abundance that didn't need even dreams.

'Why are minds like this?' But this cannot be real. The borders must be meeting somewhere. If not, how is it that I feel like I was wearing a fragrant blossom in my hair and taking the cool breeze even now? How is that possible? For sure, this happiness can never be ugly!

And then she would gently shake her lover awake. 'Get up,' she said, 'I have to go. I want to greet my husband when he comes home with jasmine blooms. And I want to light oil lamps . . . arrange them . . . sit in that light and sew the buttons on my husband's shirts.'

'Perhaps the most beautiful things are also the saddest,' her father used to say. 'No relationship can be caged in a square shape. The bonds that hold us are like flowers that bloom anywhere. That alone is their beauty. And all we can hope for are such flowers.' That pleasant evening in which Acchan said that, slowly chewing betel, was forever treasured in a pleasing corner of her mind.

When her uncle died, Saraswathi had watched from high above—the third storey of the family homestead—how Kunhilakshmi Amma stood beside her man's lifeless body, lost and even superfluous. How she lingered wordless, tearless, in the yard, and then walked away alone like a sad burnt pyre. I should have smiled at her and touched her hand reassuringly when she stood alone in the boundless emptiness.

But Saraswathi began to clearly understand square shapes when she chanced upon Ammini *cheriyamma*, her widowed aunt, her mother's younger sister, sitting with Acchan's feet on her lap; her eyes welling. Her aunt leapt up, seeing her. And walked away silently. The whole day through, Saraswathi wandered in their garden. She pulled the dried shells off the *achinga*-peas. Broke the low-lying branches of trees noisily. Kicked away the mango seeds and coconut fronds. But the glint of those teary eyes didn't disappear.

At night, Saraswathi went to her aunt who lay in bed all alone in the darkness under the wooden ceiling with her eyes wide open.

'Here are some kaitha flowers,' she offered. 'I got it from the Meledathu house . . . their garden.'

'Saraswathi,' her aunt exclaimed. 'Saraswathi!'

They sat together for some time in the dark without seeing each other's faces.

She had not yet set down the heavy heart of that night.

There was something strangely common to the stunned silence that had taken over her sister's—edathy's—face when she stared unbelievingly at her dead son, found hanging, and the smile on Saraswathi's husband's face when she fed him with loving insistence. Like the resemblance between the bigger and smaller petals of the same flower. Somewhere, the square shapes were beginning to have no boundaries at all.

As she laid her little son on her lap—he had jerked awake at night and was bawling—and rocked him back to sleep; she gently poked her husband, who was sleeping next to her. He woke.

He looked dazed at the sight of her face, which looked like frothy moonlight. She ran her fingers gently through his hair and whispered, 'Go back to sleep.'

'Sleep,' she said again. 'I woke you for nothing.'

('Chathurangal', 1977)

# Spelling Mistakes

We were sitting by the bend in the river where it curved into a half circle, where boulders lay strewn all over. Just me and Govindan. Behind the river and us, the paddy fields rose lush and verdant. The sunlight was like a clear, clean sheath. Above the cool, tranquil face of dusk, which lay on its arm, the sky was serene.

'This is my first time here,' said Govindan. 'You've been here before, eh, Suma?'

'Many times.'

'With Dinesh?'

I threw Govindan a look.

'Yes.' I twisted a blade of grass on my finger, 'Yes.'

'Don't see him these days?' He asked slowly, gently lifting the edge of the saree that was getting soaked by the water bobbing above the line of rocks. 'It's getting wet!'

'Hmm,' I said. 'Can't say a lot. But I do meet him.' When I last saw him, Dinesh had changed drastically. There was the weariness of a lifetime in those greyed temples and his moustache was now bereft of black dye. I was standing at the bus stop; he grabbed the bundle of papers I was holding and invited me to go with him to the riverside right then.

'No,' I said. 'Not in the mood somehow.'

He didn't respond. It was as if he didn't notice the people at the bus stop or our common acquaintances.

'Aparna is dead.' He said that as though his mind was flailing inwardly. Yesterday . . .'

Aparna was his oldest daughter. His favourite child.

I stepped out of the queue for the bus. And remembered with a jolt that I had forgotten the names of his other children. I couldn't even remember how many children he had.

'Come,' I said when we reached the secluded corner of the maidan. 'Let us sit down here.'

We didn't utter a word as we walked here. So, I took Dinesh's hand in mine; he sat with his head bent, wordless. He didn't pull it away or look around in fright like he did usually. Instead, he let his hand rest inside mine; we sat there for a long time. It reminded me of our evenings in the past. We didn't speak a single word about Aparna, even formally. I saw his eyes well.

Probably because I didn't know her at all—the tears didn't touch me the least. I felt a kind of fear towards my mind, which stood still, impassionate like a mere spectator. I now wondered if I should tell Govindan all of this.

'Good,' Govindan said, 'That was right. Good to hear that.'

I was sitting on the sand below, next to him. Govindan stretched his hand out towards some of my curls, which had escaped in the wind, and tucked them behind my ear.

'Weaknesses should be forgiven, Sumae,' he said as though he were completing a sentence. 'That should be the beauty of any relationship.'

Dinesh never used to sit on that rock. He always lay flat on his back, his head resting on a rock in the middle of the shrubbery beside the water.

I'd look at him when he lay like that; never did I think that we would part. A lover of my age. Dinesh would become livid hearing the word 'lover'. He thought it was degrading. I found his reaction funny, so I'd repeat it. We fell in love like divers plunging into the deep. We would feel the water surging up our noses right up to our forehead, flooding our eyes. But like the life that rolled back, the faces that shone, the coolness that enveloped one when emerging from the deep, love wrapped itself around us.

'What is its name?' asked Dinesh.

'It has no name,' I remember saying once as I reclined by the river. 'It needs no name, either.'

My little son was playing in the sand, a little away from us.

I noticed, suddenly, that Dinesh's attention was fixed on the child.

'So, you won't tell me,' he said. 'It's this secrecy that I don't like.'

When I met Dinesh, I was the unmarried mother of a two-year-old child. I didn't tell him who Vinod's father was. 'A totally irrelevant piece of information,' I said. 'Nothing special, really.' In truth, I didn't care about a name. But when he began to insist, I too became stubborn.

Then, when the evening conversations began to be invariably reduced to Vinod, I began to tire. Full of statements in which one had to cool down, boil and reduce, measure out, and cut carefully. And spaces, with clearly marked boundaries. It was suffocating. I gasped for air as though someone had pulled filthy clothes over my head.

'Vinod is my son,' I would say. 'Not anybody else's.'

'If he is to be my son too, I must know who his father is,' Dinesh panted.

I don't know what riled me so badly then—his unnecessarily angry face, his sense of entitlement that bordered on a threat, or those boxed-in evenings.

'No use,' I told him very calmly. 'You will not know it. Nor will you be his father, ever.'

He stared into the bottomless calm in my voice for some time. It was seven years since we first met. He was probably aching to start a family. His anger was probably justified. But I simply was not ready.

'Can't do without a label, uh?' I asked him one day when I was lying on his lap. 'Surely, this isn't something that you don't have to store away in the right place on some shelf?'

That made him angry. He pushed my head off his lap and stormed off into the pouring rain. I stood by the window, watching him, watching him passively. The burgeoning darkness was just a finger's length away. I ran my fingers through my hair involuntarily. With a mild smile, I feel, when I recall it now. 'Won't draw square shapes from the lines I draw,' said I; 'No harm at all doing that,' said he.

'Labels are very convenient,' Dinesh insisted. 'There's no harm at all in knowing that chilli is chilli.'

'Who has to know?' I retorted. 'I don't need labels to know.'

Vinod stood confused and stunned in the middle of this muddled and hostile air.

'Sumae, you value this bastard more than *our* life together!' He snarled.

'Hmm.' I hummed—and it felt milder and milder still when I remembered it later. I covered my mind with that hum like one would cover a knife wound running down one's spine with the palm of one's hand.

'*Our* . . .?' I asked, after a long time, in panting silence. 'Who all are included in this "our"?'

Dinesh paced the room. I took Vinod inside and put him to bed. He came over, sat on the arm of my chair, and hugged me apologetically. For the first time, lying in his arms made me afraid. And was that feeling just fear? I don't know. Out there, beyond the window, it was darkness that confronted my eyes. A faint beam of light reached right up to my feet from Vinod's room. Dinesh slept off, his head on my lap. It was some time then that I took that final decision. Later, it was in my presence that Dinesh decided to marry.

'Why not?' I asked him, without stopping for even a moment, still stirring the pan in which my curry was cooking. Maybe that was because I expected it. Or maybe because I felt that his decision was a fair one.

'He must have got married as an act of revenge,' Govindan said. 'You can well see, Suma.'

'I am not blaming Dinesh,' I clarified quickly. 'Just saying, each one knows best what they seek.'

'Your voice is turning bitter,' Govindan observed.

'Naturally,' I said, leaning on his thigh from where I sat. 'I am talking of a lover.'

'And so, Dinesh got married,' he said, running his fingers through my hair. 'Dinesh, the deep-sea diver.'

'There was nothing unnatural about it, Govinda,' I intercepted. Utterly natural, one ought to say. Something that brought relief actually.

'The relief that I didn't impede someone or stand in their way because I saw the world through my tinted glasses.'

'Dinesh did keep meeting you after, Sumae?'

'Many times. The husband has many commitments to his wife and children. Especially husbands like him, who are armed with pieces of chalk all the time to draw lines and mark off time and space. But our evenings continued to bloom and turn rosy in the open lands, free of the trash of domestic burdens and responsibilities.'

'Don't tell me that you don't know of the importance of labels, Sumae.' Govindan's words sounded like a mild scolding. 'You are old enough to know it.'

'Dinesh has reached that age too.' And then, suddenly, I said, my voice sounding torn and ragged, 'I felt as though I had fallen off a rope on which I had climbed to a great height.'

'Measure a love by what it leaves behind in you,' Govindan turned my face towards his serene, mature face. 'Not by what it lacked.' I did not wipe my overflowing tears. 'You can flow like another river.'

bothering to even glance at the idol. What to do about it, I had no clue. We just talked non-stop as we walked. We must have been gripped by the fear that if we stopped, silence would shove itself into the space between us and settle there permanently. To keep me happy, he shrewdly kept his family out of all of our conversations. And when a reference was inevitable, he made sure that it was loveless and looked accidental. I didn't know how to get rid of the weariness that grew, like mould, right through the parallel lines he drew, and my gratitude to him for those. Maybe it was the helplessness, or Dinesh stepping gingerly between the lines, or my own mind in which bubbles rose and burst—I almost said, let us end these fake walks. But then swallowed those words like vomit held back. Then, one day, I clasped his hand, very gently. That was during the daytime, in full public view. He pulled it away as though he had touched slime. And looked around frantically. That was expected, of course, but I could not take that act and that frantic look. Is 'take' the right word? It was—unpleasant, like curdled milk in one's mouth. The next day, when I asked Dinesh if he could divorce his wife, it was like trying to grab the froth of the immense wave of hate and contempt that rose in me. To this day, I don't know why I asked that—when that wasn't even in my wildest dreams. I still remember feeling like a child which had thrown away a toy and was now, for some other reason, fretting to get it back.

'I would have,' he replied. 'But there has to be a good reason?'

I stopped in my tracks as though the mud had splattered on my clothes. Is that reason more important than *our* life, I didn't ask. I rolled that totally irrelevant question like a dice in front of that smooth talk, which was now disrespectfully scratched on top of a whole life. In those walks through the maidan, it was the word 'we' that faded slowly like a sun-bleached dye. When I stood there blankly like a spectator, staring at Dinesh who was struggling to stand up straight in the middle of the blood-splattered lines, I wondered if I should tell him of this. But he did know of it. He must have seen the astonishment on my face. He smiled. I was gripped with fear—as though someone with whom one had walked miles suddenly turned around to face you, and you saw that they had a totally different face. And then, as though filling the cracks in my fissured mind, I shoved that knowledge and that fear into it.

'It's the kids . . . who are the . . . problem,' he said, as we sat side by side, bodies pressing, he caressing my midriff. He was quite sincere.

'And the "reasons" as well!' I laughed out loud, taking his hand and moving it away from my body. I have always wondered how the words that we utter without much mental preparation sometimes manage to present our thoughts with wonderful simplicity. He must have been perfectly right. It's easier to draw lines than to erase them. There is a certain orphaned feeling that overcomes us when we stand outside the boundary lines. A certain fatherlessness.

'It intoxicates some,' said Govindan. 'And it is a loss of face for others. But it is no crime.'

'True,' I said, lying down on the sand, hands under my head. 'But then individual lives will have to part. We will have to accept it as natural as hair falling. Govinda, there is nothing to replace strong self-realization and our needs that touch the bone. When he came to give me news of Aparna's death, Dinesh didn't pull away his hand though I took it in public—in daylight.'

'That's one side of the coin,' Govindan's voice grew unpleasantly heavy. 'You didn't see Dinesh flailing between his own desires and your stubbornness. You saw only the borders and boundaries. Sumae, it was the need that made those lines so important to him.' He paused. 'Dinesh loved you greatly, Sumae.'

Dinesh and I have made love on this very riverside. In the abundance of wind and rain, in the shining and endless richness of the noon. I moistened my lips which turned dry again and again even in the kindly moist dusk. 'It was true that I was very angry. Did Dinesh really think that I had seen, noticed, nothing? These doubts—persistent doubts—soil the edges of love, Govinda, like the dirt on the edges of a mundu tied too low.'

When he drew me close, Govindan seemed to be gathering in a heap a bagful of rosary peas scattered all over.

'Try some other colours,' he suggested mischievously. 'Maybe Dinesh thought that you were drawing just the tree without seeing the woods. To grow is to become capable of seeing both. It is hard for anyone to live with a face drawn by someone else.'

I saw his gentle, serene face through a film, in a blur. Like sprays of rain falling on parched earth. And then the layers of his breath right above my mind, and beyond his shoulder, the sky that had so often gazed down at me, and at which I had gazed so much. Like the burned wings of Sampathi, who had tried to fly high, and failed, I got up from the side of that river that lay still in the arms of the wind, with difficulty, almost needing a stick to haul myself up. Flecks of fatigue fell off me like blobs of earth pressed down on plant roots falling off. Once again—a journey. Not the last, perhaps—of the abiding ties exacted by life's paths.

('Aksharathettukal', 1992)

# Definitions in Different Hues

Salini lingered near the door. Vasu ettan was asleep with one leg on the cot, foot pressed on the mattress, knee raised, the other leg flung across the rest of the space, his mouth slightly ajar. His usual sleeping pose of many years.

Usually, she would go up to him, lower and straighten the leg gently, set the pillow right, and cover him with the blanket. But Salini did not move; she kept looking. Then, as though flicking something off her mind, she went up and extricated the other pillow from beneath his head carefully without waking him.

Not sure why, but she didn't want to sleep on that bed.

Not just this time but for many days now.

This reluctance was a bit like the thin film of dust that collects on the surface of a table. She couldn't recall when it had grown so pronounced. Press the finger on it now—there would be a distinct mark. So thick it had become.

Sometimes she asked herself why not blow it away with a sharp, single puff. But what if the whole layer of dust blew right back on my face, she asked herself a counter-question. Maybe she would not recognize her own dust-covered face.

Maybe even Vasu ettan would not recognize her. And what if the smoothness and shine of the old days stared back at her from under that layer of dust? That may even frighten me, she told herself.

That was also the fear she felt these days when she looked at Vasu ettan's face. It was never there back then, at a time when she sat next to him in the south-side courtyard of the family house, and he tried to make her feel better.

It wasn't he who changed. It was me, Dr Salini.

'Salu, do you want to study more?'

Vasu ettan once surmounted Grandmother's declaration that the family had no resources to send her to faraway places to study nor was she getting any younger for it.

'So? Are you going to educate me, Vasu etta?' She had burst out.

He didn't reply. Only caressed her head with a smile.

The truth was that when she walked towards the path that made her Dr Salini holding onto Vasu ettan's hand, she had not even dreamt of such slow-sedimenting grime.

From that day onwards, he's been protecting me like a flame kept alive by protecting palms, she thought. Whenever I turned back to think, it was like I was a precious gift to him. What he had desired but never achieved, he readied for Salini. I was to him a continuation of his life.

He stood on the doorstep of my world of research— of the lab, the seminars, the lecture notes, the questions, the hypotheses, the possibilities—like an unlettered father sending his child to school for the very first time. Full of adoration, pure joy. At that moment he would not have thought of the compulsions of that world or of its snares and raptures. Am I describing it right—*was it that he did not think? Or that he could not have possibly thought?* When I returned home late in the evening after my crazy busy days, struggling to gather up scattered doubts and guesses and inferences buzzing inside my head and stacking them there in some decent order, Vasu ettan would be already in bed, waiting for me. I used to be reluctant to even glance at his face those days. Not reluctance—I should say that clearly, it was guilt. That was why I tried my best to smile, even when my mind was in turmoil.

That was why I tried to shape both right and wrong with smiles.

'This is not right,' he would say when I collapsed into bed in sheer exhaustion.

'Isn't it time we had a baby?'

'That can be had any time.' That was my usual reply. In truth, each time the matter of having a baby came up, I recoiled in fear. I took care to keep it just a discussion. I know even now that Vasu ettan never pressed the matter only to keep me happy. Slowly, it began to feel like a thorn stuck inside the throat perpetually. That's why when I learnt that I was pregnant, all I could do was lean on the wall slack-jawed. My project was in a very crucial phase; the deadline looming ahead could not be moved. To step back would mean throwing out all the effort I had put into it until then, at least. But to even utter the word 'abortion' to Vasu ettan's glowing face would be cruelty, perhaps. I had no clue how I could pull it out without the leaf tearing and the thorn breaking.

'Abortion?' he yelled. 'Are you mad, Salu? True, it was unplanned. But we didn't decide against having children, did we?'

That was totally expected. Even the gesture—the hands pressed down.

'I have no answer to such questions,' I delivered the line I'd long prepared in my mind. Without looking at his face. 'Why didn't we plan for one, Vasu etta? What was the reason? Has that reason disappeared suddenly?'

'I am not trying to assert my right or power,' he got up suddenly. 'Just tell me—is our life to be lived according to Dr Salini's wishes alone?'

That question hit me, many parts of me, like a lit firecracker thrown hard.

How selfish someone can get, Vasu ettan must have thought. Isn't motherhood important to her, he must have wondered. My answer is clear: no, it is not.* Whatever the Puranas and Vedas may say, my happiness is clearly in completing my project. It was because I said this openly that Saraswathi Amma and Poduvaal who were having lunch with me froze—and stared—like they had seen a ghost, the rice balls in their fingers hovering in mid-air.

Not sure if it was to convince myself that this was not just selfishness or to establish that I would not be defeated by this attitude—I didn't abort Balu. Instead, I vented it on Sudhir—like one flings away a poem one wrote, struck out, rewrote, struck out again, until it made one dizzy. 'Stop it, Sudhir,' I snapped. 'This isn't

---

* No use hanging on my neck such words as 'wifehood' and 'motherhood'. The truth is that I am not touched by them in the least.

something you'd understand. Human bonds have their needs too.'

'Yes, I agree,' he said, switching the pump on and directing it towards the glass bulb. 'Your life is fruitful! Why do you need the project now?' From his look, it seemed as though the words 'gratitude', 'defeat', 'love', and 'selfishness' were turning round and round inside the glass bulb like in a pulverizer. The acid that bubbled at the head of the funnel looked like his yellowed smile.

'If the responsibility is yours, the decision should be yours too.' He said, 'You must know at least that much.'

'I'm not asking for a justification,' I retorted. 'I'm asking for a solution.'

'You're asking for a shortcut, Salini.' His voice grew heavier.

'Those who get a high from their inner lives are always going to be cast out. No point pretending that you don't know that.'

When your mind is fermenting over, full of ire, you would be scared even to take a firm stride—why doesn't anyone notice that? If you do, what's inside then splashes on others around you; it dirties the floor . . . All the time when I nursed Balu, changed his nappies, gave him a bath, the fluid in the glass bulb inside my head bubbled up with renewed determination.

This was why I decided to go back to work two weeks after Balu's birth. There was a hint of contrition in my hiring Mrs D'Souza to take care of him at double the wage.

And maybe, a dash of revenge as well.

'Just fifteen days for him,' Vasu ettan begged, sounding scalded. 'Who'll care for him?' That question, which I had asked myself again and again, to absolute exhaustion. 'I don't want questions, Vasu etta, I want answers.'

'Let him grow up a little. The project can wait.'

Was it that he didn't understand? I froze in my steps and stared at him. Or maybe insisting that he won't understand? If you think that the weakness is that I have given birth, then you're mistaken.

I won't bend.

When I closed the zip of the cover of the feeding bottle with a decisive movement of my fingers and handed Balu to Mrs D'Souza, Vasu ettan stood there looking at me as though he had seen some stranger.

No. I am not sad at all.

It was not right or wrong, it was necessary. Earlier he used to tell me—comb your hair a bit, won't you, before you leave? Instead, now his eyes searched the strands of my hair, which were starting to grey, in the dark circles spreading around my eyes, and my thick spectacles. The distance between the Salu who would take a bath and freshen up before running up with a smile, and this woman who was running towards the door after hurriedly handing the child to the ayah must have stumped him too. I, too, am beginning to tire of the endless, indelible pain and helplessness on Vasu ettan's face.

That's why I am still holding back the news of the fellowship and the trip abroad from him, though it has been three weeks since it was announced.

I am going to go, for sure.

I walked all this way for journeys like this.

Against that firmness, when Vasu ettan stands there like a hearth full of smouldering coals and scattering sparks, I will have to ignore the things that the heat turns to soot.

They are like the dust that soils the feet, the pain in the limbs—all that which have to be borne in a journey, I do think.

Poduvaal, while processing my papers for the trip abroad, had spat hard, 'The ungrateful wretch! She's grown big on his expense and now can't stand him. The ingrate!'

I wanted to ask Poduvaal—is it possible for someone to keep on expressing one's gratitude for the whole of one's life?

But Grandmother too had said, do not rub the oil on your hair unmindful of the head. Not just her, but also Rajani, Saraswathi Amma, and Panikkar. Words like thin straight lines, so like tightropes stretched above abysses. So narrow, one misstep will fling you into the depths.

I stopped and sighed hard into my chest. Knowing what you want to wipe off from your mind is actually scarier.

Vasu ettan was sleeping.

Maybe he too will stand here, by the door, look at the bed like this and think: Salu, could you have not told me a word about this trip?

And could you not have given me at least a word of gratitude?

'In what words am I to express it all, Vasu etta?'

'Here, when I pick up this pillow, when I lie down, when I take a bath—I am searching for those words, all the time.'

Those words are the colour of the termite-eaten debris, falling out of the mind when the face of the feverish baby in Mrs D'Souza's arms appears like a spark above my rows of equations and my writing.

Vasu ettan, too, will feel that the moonlit path of the past, the coolness that lingered in the feet, or the radiance of lit minds will not be enough; that they all give off a slightly burned smell.

Sudhir often says that life is a place where the logic and conclusion of the days of experiment do not work. Let me, for now, borrow those words.

('Nirvanchanangalude Nirabhedangal', 1995)

# The Seasons

Pushing her husband's leg off her body, she sat up. It was very dark all around. In front of her was a small square of brightness drawn by the faint light that had entered from the street.

The regular ebb and flow of long breaths. His face was vague in the darkness. But even the shape of his nose was sharply etched in her heart. Not moving their entwined arms, she caressed her sleeping husband's head and wondered: why is this? It's bad. This habit. Sitting up at midnight and thinking of random things. Not reaching anywhere, ending up with even more tangled knots. In the end, when she slipped into sleep leaning on the headboard of the bed, when she woke up late in the morning, only fatigue and irritation would remain.

She sat there quietly, running her fingers on her half-opened mouth, her smooth stomach. Pure insolence like her aunt used to say long back. This is the trouble when everything goes perfectly, she would remark. Look at her strut. What in heaven does she lack, really?

Long, luxuriant tresses, lightly tied at the tip. Eyes lined with kohl; the spot of kumkum on the forehead. Each time she felt smaller and flustered in front of the love that held her close. The love that lined her eyes with kohl whenever she forgot it. She tried to add up. Where did it go wrong?

The sanctity of the temple, the sincerity of the praying man. Once he said: To get the chance to love that which we adore . . . that's what one needs luck for. She was lying with her head on her husband's chest as he said it. His slender, smooth fingers ran gently all over her body. Lovingly, as if he were caressing a flower. Somewhere behind her eyes, the tears sprang up. They simmered within, unable to break out. Drawing on his stubbly beard with her forefinger, she had told him that day: I know now what beauty is and what happiness is.

He kissed her on the parting of her hair and held her hand firmly. But when she remembered the cold indifference of her body—how it was so then as it is now, she corrected herself. No. I wasn't lying then. But as she stood helpless before that sentence that could never be completed, she heard the voice of her husband's heart with utmost clarity. Her heart, however, was unclear.

Rubbing the end of her braided hair on his cheek, he laughed, 'You are lukewarm, girlie!' She quickly grasped what he meant. It was always this way. Not disappointed, not angry, he let himself be conquered by it. Whenever she teetered between helplessness and anger, her husband's voice sounded pathetic. In trying to affirm love, she thought, I am losing the little I have. It was no one's fault. There was a time when she watched a man, someone who looked after the farm back home, walk into the narrow path behind the cowshed leading to the fields; it made her heart pound in her ears. The sight of the white shirt approaching from the distance would make the pores of her body burst into bloom. She thought that her quivering legs might give way if their eyes met . . . the thrill of it! That thrill must have fallen off in some little bylane of the past. She never found it again. The bunch of kaitha flowers thrown under the fence, slipped under watching eyes, was far prettier to her than any of the gifts she had received in the past four years. Then, when she gazed beyond the rolling paddy fields unable to even move an eyelid, her mind was light. Only that the sight of the blue pea flower's smile blooming against a sheet of full and brilliant sunlight seemed very beautiful.

Those evenings in which cheeks, flushed when their garments had brushed against each other near the clump of bamboo, peeped in the mirror. Mornings in which one smiled at the tiny doves in their nests while drawing water from the well.

'Uh?'

The bedroom lamp brightened.

'Uh?' More anxiety than lingering sleep.

'Where is the blanket? I am cold.'

He held her close and whispered in her ear: 'Why do you need a blanket for that?'

She felt utterly furious with herself—not even a pore had stirred.

'I am sleepy.' She blurted out.

A second. At the end of a sigh, he held her hands even more. Then, caressing her eyelids, he said: 'Sleep.'

As she closed her eyes praying for the sleep that was never to come, the man's heartbeat destroyed her peace. Her own heart, pounding extraordinarily. She was filled with disgust. The insides of her eyelids were hollows, bereft of dreams. She opened her eyes out of fear, disgust. When she turned like she was in sleep, she noticed a part of that hairy chest. The arm around her was still tight. In front of her now was a wall on which darkness was pasted. Why was her heart pounding so, she thought. Why aren't the kids in the next room screaming? Mirages, all. The inside of one set of four walls was the same as the inside of another such set. Oh, only if the milkwoman came soon. In the light of the bedroom lamp, the shape of the flowers on the table is that of a camel. Inside the wardrobe, many empty hangers. The ever-smiling Sreekrishna statuette in front of the bronze lamp. As her eyes wandered aimlessly, she wished again fervently. If the milkwoman came, the pots and pans in the kitchen will stir awake. This will end in the faint and pleasant light of dawn. This suffocation.

The unending ticking of the clock. With unbearable disgust, she switched off the light. It was just two o'clock at night. Hours to go. So many hours to go before dawn. She turned away from the tears that had fallen on the satin pillowcase and pressed her hand on her husband's cheek. 'Come,' she said, wiping off the wetness of her tears. 'I am not sleepy at all.'

('Ritukkal', 1972)

except on her breast, she wouldn't recognize it, even. For a second, she felt that she should shove that by now enormous head off her body and scream loudly. But at the same time, she should not wake him. It may be rather mean to push away a man sleeping with his head on her breast with a serenity bordering on childlike innocence. That would be ineffaceable shame on her womanhood and her father's honour. And besides, avoidable trouble—for someone like her who had not yet sought another means to placate hunger. Just when this thought struck her, the peacock above raised itself on one leg and turned in a circle. Its long feathers brushed hard on the man's body and her face. That's how its feathers began to be covered with pus and germs, like ancient dust that drowned and dimmed its colours. She remembered the wandering *Kurathy* woman, who read her palm during the temple fair, had predicted: 'Your fate is to bear the weight of a mighty man's head on your breast.' It made her jump up, screaming. Because the soft breast beneath his head slipped off unexpectedly, he too started awake.

She withdrew into a corner in fear, expecting the reddish flash of anger from within those heavy-drooping eyelids that were slowly opening now. The sour, rancid bile provoked by the unbearable odour of ill health that pervaded the room filled her mouth now; it dribbled out despite her best efforts to hold it back and soaked the edge of her saree with which she had covered her mouth, out of fear and respect.

'O Divine Lord! My God,' she said (the fluid still seeping out of her mouth), 'I beg you, pardon me! Save this *patrivrata*, given entirely to the worship of her husband! I do not even know where this disgusting bitter water in my mouth comes from.'

'Sheelavathi,' he called when he was finally fully awake in a low, stern voice. 'This deed of yours was totally inappropriate. Who does it bring shame to? It is no adornment to any wife . . .'

'Yes, My Lord, yes,' agreed Sheelavathi hurriedly, not letting him complete his statement. 'Please forgive me! It is a great honour that you bestowed on me when you made me your wife! But truly, I am not worthy of it! I am an unfortunate being who does not deserve it.'

Sheelavathi's man looked at her with compassionate eyes and remained thoughtful.

'My dear,' he said. 'It is not the place of the wife that matters—do not be beguiled by ornamentation. I find my wings in the sweetness of your poetry, in the gentle grace of your anklets, in the modesty of your mellifluous words. You are my treasure.'

Is the sourness in my mouth actually sweet now? Sheelavathi could not help doubting. Lowering her long eyelids bashfully, she slowly swallowed it. She sat down, took the legs he had swung towards the floor on her lap, and began to press them tenderly as though she was a tanpura player absorbed in her music. Are the strains of music scattering around us? And then, loosening her luxuriant tresses, Sheelavathi wiped off the pus and other vile secretions from his diseased feet.

Running his fingers on her full bust as though on a sceptre, throwing a benevolent look with his hallowed eyes at her lovely navel, which shone like a beautiful pendant on a waist-belt, His Majesty The Man looked pleased.

'Alright,' he ordered, 'bring the basket.'

The hands gently stroking his leg paused momentarily on the parched, rough skin. Sheelavathi had studied about leprosy as a communicable disease and how it was transmitted as a student of the eighth standard. So, she reminded herself that she must wash everything from the tip of her tresses to her body, and even her mind, in diluted Dettol.

She brought the basket only after scrubbing herself well.

Sheelavathi lifted the basket on her head and walked through the street trodden by many before her. Following her Guru's instructions, she had lined the insides and edges of the basket with soft, fresh leaves so that it would be cool. She walked and walked— through bylanes lined with pea flower vines in full bloom, through dense forests, on the banks of the ocean. She walked as slowly as she could, fearing that the body of The Man who, like an idol, sat inside the basket that she carried on her head would ache. And also to not let him sense her fatigue.

'Do your feet ache?' he asked. 'Your tender feet deserve slippers made of flowers!'

Licking off the sweat that ran down from her brow, Sheelavathi smiled. 'How lucky am I!' And walked even more carefully, slowly.

'The tinkle of your anklets,' he said, 'titillates not just me but all of nature. I am greatly roiled by that stag who stands there looking at you. Are you returning his gaze, my beloved, *priye*?'

'No,' she said, pulling her gaze abruptly off that spotted deer who had mesmerized Seetha, Lord Srirama's wife. 'I don't even see it.' She laughed, sounding like pearls falling and rolling on the ground.

'Oh, how wary you sound!' she teased, feeling proud. 'Ah! My dance, my song, my body, my love—I am fulfilled, my Lord!'

But it was with no forewarning at all that he then began to howl. Sheelavathi was completely taken aback seeing The Man writhe and flay, trying to get out of his basket.

'Bring it down, bring down the basket,' he snarled. A little ahead of them walked a well-born woman with long, lovely waves of hair falling to her knees, streaks of sandalwood paste on her forehead, followed by two *dasi* women. She suddenly stopped, stupefied, in the shade of a huge tree and leaned on its trunk—seeing her son and Sheelavathi.

'Amma!' He clambered out of the basket with difficulty, lisping with fear and surprise.

'Yes, so what?' Sheelavathi said with some irritation, rubbing her foot, which was a bit sprained when the Man struggled hard to get out of the basket. 'Go, pay your respects to her.'

He stared at Sheelavathi's face for some time like a madman. And drawing out a sweetness and humility that she had never heard until then, he begged, 'Please, Sheelavathi, why don't you move into the shade of that bower and hide for some time? Rest for a while? I know that your legs must be aching from all the walking. Let me pacify Amma?'

'You coward . . .' Forgetting the downy feathers that lined the basket, the unbearable pain in her foot, and the strained muscles of her neck, she shouted again, 'Coward!'

And then, facing The Man's brows shaping into a frown, wiping off the sweat from her brow with the saree's edge, she laughed so loud that The Man, Amma, and Earth itself shook.

'This . . .' he spoke in a tone that suited a matured soul, 'This does not suit any well-born bride . . . You who have mastered the fine arts, you who know of life's ways, you should not behave like a stubborn little girl.

'Stop laughing so loud and try to understand,' he added in an irate voice as if recalling something.

He prostrated at his mother's feet. Sheelavathi went into the shade of the bower, sat down, and pulled out a thorn that had pierced her foot during the long walk. She pressed down her ankle on the ground and rubbed it hard. Spat hard and wiped off the spittle around her mouth. Through a small gap between the vines of the bower, she peeped at the mother and son. At that moment Sheelavathi had forgotten all that her mother had taught her about the qualities of worthy well-born women. And so she eavesdropped; sharpened her ears to catch as much as she could of the conversation.

'My son,' his mother sobbed, 'is this your bride? This?'

'No,' the son was sorrowful. 'You, who raised me, Amma, you should never have asked me that question.'

'My son,' Mother said, 'it is a sin to die without having sons. Your duty is to find a suitable mate like all other living beings and produce offspring through her. Do not become an insult to your lineage by remaining without sons. Amma cannot bear it. Find a well-born bride to serve you and your children.'

The son sat with his head bent. Sheelavathi, too, was convinced of everything the mother said. She parted the vines once again to get a better look.

The Man did not glance at the bower even once; he fixed his eyes on his mother with a pitiful expression. He began to say something but stopped halfway.

'Son,' continued the Mother, 'The fear that this woman of yours may weep is misplaced. Maybe she will, being so young. But your ascent to heaven will convince her of how trivial her feelings are. It is through more and more of such selfless thoughts that she shall rise to maturity and security. She will then shine like a piece of gold in the fire, like Seetha after her trial by fire. You were just three days old when your father brought his second wife into our bedchamber. That day I vacated the marriage bed like a respectable, well-born woman. And your father was so pleased with me that he sent me through the servant a necklace of diamonds he had bought for my co-wife. Here, look, I have never taken it off my neck after that.' Mother showed her son the sparkling pendant on her neck. Sheelavathi thought, just like this mother, her mother too had given her the same advice: 'If you pull out a pole from a burning house, that's profit!'

Amma was putting on her neck a gold necklace, the first gift The Man had brought her—she was then a virgin.

'Daughter,' she said, 'Don't be a fool ever. Next time, tell him you want a chain that falls below your breasts. You know that long gold chain design called "November's Loss"? Get one of those chains. That will suit you well. You should tell your bridegroom that.'

He brought beautiful chains that reached under her breasts, just above her navel. But Sheelavathi was not too keen on these. She was tired and nauseous with morning sickness. One day, when she woke, she found a glittering, gem-encrusted sword by her bedside. Sheelavathi's mother stroked her hair and forehead slowly. 'It's a gift from him,' said she. 'My dear, it is a gift to your son about to be born from his father; his father's name is to be kept a secret from him, too . . .'

Before her mother could complete that sentence, Sheelavathi had seized the sword and brought it down with full force on her mother's neck. She stepped across her mother's corpse, which was now cut in two; clutching the bloodied sword, she strode towards the king's residence. She had forgotten to tie up her hair, which lay loose, reaching her ankle; her clothes were in disarray. Because a beautiful young woman could not be striding thus in the streets without some reason, and because it was necessary to protect the good name of the masters, the servants closed all the doors and windows of the royal durbar hall as soon as she stepped in.

'Where is my husband, O Rajan?' she asked.

'Beautiful one,' the King, completely taken by her beauty and sweet tone, asked, 'Who?'

"My husband,' she snapped. 'The father of my child.'

'Where is your *thali*, your marriage locket?' growled a Brahmin who stood there looked dumbfounded, as though he were insulted. 'Why it there no sindoor in the parting of your hair?'

She saw him just then; the sword was still in her hand. She threw it to him, panting hard: 'Why do my child or I need a sword? These are for you, Your Grace. People like me need your name. Your presence.'

'Do you know her?' the King intervened.

'Rajan,' he cleared his throat a couple of times. 'I did not recognize her first. Forgive me. But the sword made me remember her, like a signet ring.'

'And then?' the King asked.

'She is accomplished in all the arts, intelligent, and as you can see, beautiful.' He paused. 'Someone who can turn the whole world into a sheet of silver with her dazzling smile. She who filled my nights with moonlight. But Rajan, you surely know. We cannot make her the mother of our heirs. She is the daughter of the court dancer.' He then turned towards Sheelavathi. 'Beloved, you must understand. This relationship I, a Brahmin, have with you is not allowed in the society protected by Kings or sanctioned by the Vedas! In return for the heavenly pleasures you gave me, you will have a son as bright as the sun. No. Do not weep. Do not gaze at me with your tear-filled eyes, which are as beautiful as the lotus wet with dew.'

'In the first place,' interjected another Brahmin who was sitting next to him, 'is there any evidence that this woman's child is indeed yours? This is the sort of woman who wanders the streets to mislead men with the temptations of sin.'

Sheelavathi, quite contrary to her name, grew furious. 'If the child is not his,' she declared, 'let him prove it.'

Everyone, including the King, fell senseless as though struck by lightning. Nothing of this sort was ever heard in any *nitisara*. Uttered, quite shamelessly, by a slip of a girl! That, too, one who ought to be like a vine hanging heavy with fruit, a woman who should look down, mindful of the fullness of her breasts.

It was the King who awoke first from that fit of unconsciousness; he ordered that she be bound like a wild beast.

'Desist!' the Protector of the People said, his eyes on his own feet, not her face. 'That your eyes fall on me is an insult to me. The arrogance manifest in your determination to question this great man who had adorned your bed many times, in front of all these great souls well-versed in the arts of duty and justice, dharma and *neethi*—it is a slur on the face of all womenfolk and my country. Therefore, you will be thrown with your full belly to the lions.'

When it became clear that death was the only destination, Sheelavathi was flustered. Even if it were because of her child's father, dying at eighteen seemed rather unnecessary to her.

'Rajan,' she now began. 'Forgive me please, my ignorance, my pettiness. Not just my mother but even Queen Draupadi had indeed taught me that some questions should never be asked in front of even the greatest of souls. You are merciful, like God himself. Please forgive the child in my womb, the son of this illustrious man, even though I am his mother. I will never tell him his father's name. He, too, may not forgive his mother who besmirched his father's name. Lord, bless my son so he may grow strong like Jamadagni's son Parasurama.'

'Beautiful one,' the King relented, 'I forgive your mutinous words uttered negligently. But, pretty wench, now that you are pregnant, won't you have to stay away from song and dance for some time?'

'Ah!' cried Sheelavathi. 'Do you not worry about this miserable creature's life! I am gratified! My Man, who is the very adornment of this durbar, will not forsake me. It is my privilege to wear at the parting of my hair as sindoor the dust of his feet.'

The King's eyes filled with tears of joy. He said, 'Sheelavathi, take care of your Man; serve his every need. Be his consolation, as a mother to a child, as a pleasure-woman to a man. To make sure that his diseased body does not ache, carry him in the basket, in your indulgence, your pride. Sheelavathi, be his glittering adornment—shine more than your glowing face.'

That's how I got the name Sheelavathi, she remembered. Before, my name used to be Sarala or Diptha or something of that sort.

On the other side of the bower, the mother was beginning to weep at the prospect of her son ending up son-less.

'Amme,' he told her. 'If your tears fall, this earth will not forgive me, I know. Therefore, your son bows down and takes upon himself your wish and command.' Wiping away her tears, the mother looked at her son with shining eyes. Did any tears fall by chance on the ground, she worried a bit. Then she held him close.

'The girl who carries you around will cry like the bamboo being split,' she told him. 'Her song and dance, now wet with tears, will be as beautiful as the vines in a storm. She will twist and turn from the arms of one man to another like a cobra with a very flexible spine under a gleaming snakeskin. But she will begin to hate herself, soaked in her own venomous breath. And then, in that unbearable stance, beneath the sky, grown broad and white and ready to fall, she will stay silent, like a bullet never fired. The weight of that, my child, you will not be able to bear, being of gentle mind and bearing many responsibilities towards the world. On that day, only your wife can save you by the strength of her chastity like Savithri, who took her husband back from Yama himself. Therefore, you should choose one from among the virgins I have lined up for you. The horoscopes of these women who are well-born, who will cook the tastiest food and serve you to perfection, who are content to fill their bellies with your leftovers, who will participate like prostitutes in any kind of sex of your preference, kinky or plain, from the very first night, who will be in the day time like the touch-me-not, drooping at first sight of another man, who will never laugh or cry aloud, who will give you male progeny, who will give you as much dowry as you ask, and on top, apartments, fancy cars, and plum jobs too—these horoscopes match yours perfectly. They have been matched, as you know, by none other than our very own Raman Nair of that Vadakke house near us. He has marked the breast-waist-hips measurements of the bodies to be considered on their respective horoscopes in letters of gold. Son, get married, earn your place in heaven.'

That bevy of beauties presented themselves in a neat row, all of a sudden, like heavenly beings appearing before sages, performing rigorous penance in the mythological movies. He walked up and down the row with his swollen head and the diseased gleam on his face, inspecting each. For a moment, Sheelavathi thought: why not throw the basket in a corner and join the line? Then she decided against it. He may recognize her worn feet like notes out of key among those of her rivals, which were soft and unblemished, fresh as tender leaves, regularly rubbed with the juice of hibiscus flowers. And that may lead to her losing her good name in the royal palace.

As Sheelavathi was lost in her thoughts, he chose the youngest, coyest girl among the lot—the one whose alluring breasts heightened the loveliness of her thin upper garment—he tied the thali thread around her neck. Actually, the girl's thighs were bound together, so she could not but walk daintily like a swan. The gods rained flowers from the heavens on the sacred marriage locket, the thali.

'My daughter,' her foster father spoke in a voice quivering with emotion. 'Like Damayanti was to Nala, who abandoned her in the deep jungle to the wild beasts; like Seetha to Srirama, who saved his people and his throne that he had retaken after full fourteen years, by sending his pregnant wife to the forest, be an ornament to your husband. Remember, because your body is to be consigned to the flames of your husband's pyre, his health and longevity are of utmost importance to you. Receive his seed like the very earth. Bring his progeny into the world, suffering the pain of clipping your wings. Never fall into the fatal whirlpool of *adharma*, like that haughty Amrita Pritam who lived away from her husband, or like Karuthamma of *Chemmeen* (the novel) who let the sea swallow up Palani. His name and his family rest on your chastity.'

The wedding procession began then. Sheelavathi pulled herself back some more. In the horrible cacophony of the *nadaswaram*, the wedding band, and the shehnai, he suddenly hobbled in pain; the stumps that were his legs were scraping on the sand.

'My beloved,' he said. 'I can't walk.'

His wife saw his putrefying feet only then. She bent down, scooped up the divine soil from beneath them and wore it on her head reverentially. Suddenly, a basket sent down reverentially by angels in heaven appeared before her. Though she was a bit taken aback at first because its arrival was completely unexpected, she paid attention to what others around her were saying and proclaimed thus, 'I am indeed lucky to be able to carry you thus. Therefore, please climb into the basket. This burden is indeed my right.'

That night, after pristine sex that was not tainted by fear or doubt or the shadow of adharma, he fell into an immensely peaceful slumber. In the morning, the beauty of her naked body right by his side thrilled him again.

'Priye, my dearest,' he called to her, his voice quavering with feeling. 'Put on your anklets. Let their laughter intoxicate me.'

She was appalled. She was silent. She lowered her head before him like someone guilty.

'I don't know dance and song and chess,' she said with humility. I read only *Women's Era*, *Femina*, *Mangalam*, *Manorama*.'

'What!' he shouted, even forgetting that this was their nuptial night. 'So, all my nights, henceforth, are to be silent like this one? Oh! You did not say a word of this to me before! Do I need to tell you that the wife's duty is to find out about her husband's likes and dislikes? You could have warned the marriage broker, at least?'

'Please forgive me, my Lord,' she begged. 'These are not things suited to well-born women.'

'Who told you?' he roared again. 'I sleep to the tinkle of anklets. You must soothe me to sleep with the tanpura.'

'Lord . . .' she floundered like a trapped doe; she implored: 'Lord, you did not ask me. No one asked.

Lord, you who are proficient in the Vedas and the sciences, do not forsake an immature and ignorant girl like me. Because I have shared your bed once, I will be rejected by others like a soiled banana leaf after the feast. So, please rise. Let me carry you to that place where the magical music of anklets and the music of the tanpura may be found.'

'And so, I have reached you again,' he said, lying on Sheelavathi's lap, thinking ruefully of his wife waiting with the basket in the next room and his own faith.

She ran her fingers through his hair and was silent.

'Fate,' he continued. 'So many others were there in that row! Yet, the one who must share my bed, bear my children, bring colour and splendour to my dreams, be my abode, my refuge, my passion, my glory—she drains my days and nights of life and colour! My beloved, when I wake at night, it is your anklets and your eyes that I remember.'

She got up to dance for him like a feisty gust of breeze; the bells of her anklets sounded like a gurgling waterfall. Stepping back a moment from the vivacity of her dance and the gushing of her anklets, Sheelavathi asked him. 'Her . . .' She paused for a second. 'What's her name?'

'My wife's?' he asked.

'Sheelavathi.'

('Sheelavathi', 1983)

# The Sword of the Princess

The little flame on the lit match was like a bud about to open—close enough to touch. What if I let it bloom on the edge of my garments? My saree would start burning slowly like a bud bursting open. In the middle of the fire's beautiful leaping tongues, I will shine like the Goddess Saraswathi sitting on her blossoming lotus in the calendar that hangs in my house. The glow of the flames and their heat may even render me unconscious. And then they will surge and sway in rhythm. I may remind you then of a magnificent river that flows more or less serenely, touching both its banks. The flow and the radiance of fire have always reminded me of rippling water.

But all this will unfold this way only if I am able to attain the same grandeur and serenity as the fire that spreads around me. Maybe that is impossible for a human being. And so, quite contrary to my wishes, I may scream out loud. My husband, who will wake up rudely, will rush up here and stand rooted to the ground seeing me covered in tongues of fire. He may scramble to look for a blanket and water, cursing my carelessness inwardly. I think I am going to be really pleased to see his panic. Winning is no less than an aching need for me. I am sick of losing again and again. I need a victory over the dreams that keep me in a constant state of fear, bewilderment, helplessness and over this proud mind of mine, which keeps seeking reasons defiantly of everything—of eating or loving or whatever. I believe that this may somehow be possible when I stand in the middle of the flames. When I am beyond the grasp of my mind and my dreams, I will see on their faces, just like on my husband's face, a certain betrayed expression. Like when your prey escapes your mouth. That's when I am going to brim with happiness. None of them is going to come anywhere near this luminous heat for fear of scorching their fingers. And thus, when I get beyond them all, when I stand triumphantly, joyously, I will address the world so loud that all who can hear may hear. Why—those who love fire and its warmth cannot help loving human beings too. I have always wanted to say this from outside the narrow, shrivelled boundaries of causes and effects.

The lit match had died. The cold water atop the stove, my crumpled saree, all were the same. Only the burnt-out matchstick lay in tiny spots of black on the sides of the hearth. Then, as I slowly set the water to boil on the stove, it all began to appear unreal and unfamiliar to me. Last night, I lay all alone at the end of a long dark passage. There were no exits from that narrow space flanked by thick walls. My mind was like a piece of its smooth, polished interior—visible beneath my skin like a splinter of granite in clear water. That mind of mine lay absolutely motionless as though inside a pool, the water of which had frozen, and there was never any prospect of a ripple. I rolled on the shiny floor of that passage, from one end to another, again and again, that mind inside rolling in me. I was about to burst into wailing and weeping many times, but my voice was not even human. I stopped it; it sounded so grotesque and piercing that it could not possibly have been mine. I wanted to cry, badly wanted to cry, but I kept my mouth shut out of the fear of my voice. That's why I kept rolling up and down again. It was only after rolling over and over on the floor, up and down, for a long time, that I found that piece of iron. I picked it up and started to wound the cold faces of the walls that surrounded me. I realized that just outside those walls was my child, the world, and also many well-salted and well-spiced curries. I kept rubbing nonstop that small

I slowly opened my fingers and checked, knowing well that it was foolishness. My pretty fingers were still rosy and clean.

As soon as I reached the kitchen, I pushed open the windows forcefully, with a vengeance. The wind forced its way inside like an enemy. The presence of an enemy is so much better than being alone! Assailed by a wave of tiredness, I broke the matchstick that I had taken out and lowered myself onto a nearby stool. I think that's how I slept off again.

I woke up when I heard my husband brushing his teeth. His face was swollen with fury. I pretended not to notice. What all do I have to pretend not to notice? I must pretend not to notice my dreams, my husband's angry face, the way in which the face of the little child on the road outside below my balcony waiting for me to throw the stale chapatis turns into the face of my little boy, the flies that buzz around the head and body of my maid, who gathers the leftovers into the dirty aluminium container to feed her kids . . .

My husband had made some tea. The tea waste and the burnt bits of the matchstick still lay on the kitchen counter. I set the milk on the stove and began to pour cool water on my face, and suddenly, for no reason, the memory of the little beggar boy who resembled my little boy, Kuttan, came back again. I must tell him to come one afternoon when I am alone here. I must take him to the bathroom, give him a nice loving bath with nice soap, and new clothes to wear. And, after a sumptuous meal, take him on my lap and soothe him to sleep. And then? Let that wait, I told myself. First, what lies will work with the Gurkha guard to get the little boy in? The Gurkha will stare contemptuously. He will have to send the child in if I order him to, using all the authority that these gold ornaments that I wear bestow on me. But there will be talk. The respectable folks who live in my building will begin their lament about my willfulness and uncouth deeds. That can only be so when the standards of our respectability are with someone else. But, even if slowly, the matter will reach my husband. As I stood washing my face and thinking of all this, the milk boiled over and flowed out. I stared at the stove for a few moments and switched it off. My excessive slowness seemed to have angered my husband even more. He stood there staring at me, still holding the oil he had taken on his palms to rub on his head.

Looking at the drops of oil dripping through his fingers, acting as though nothing had happened, I said, 'Let me go out? I think I am not at all well today.'

My husband stood still, not even moving his hand. But when I passed him on my way out, he stopped me forcibly.

'Let me go,' I said. 'I will be back soon.'

But his grip grew tighter and more painful. His face seemed blackened by rage. Suddenly, with no reason at all, I began to recall that exit-less passage in which I had rolled so many times. Thinking of it later, I felt that it was from this moment that the rage began to build in me. I felt that I could shake him off easily with a sharp shrug; he was just a child, a trifle. Great contempt, anger, deep revulsion, blind strength—all of it began to spark in my mind like flares from a smouldering pit of fire falling all around.

'Let me go,' I said again. 'I'll return soon.' I saw the rosy dawn grow beyond the window. The humming of the wind began to grow in my head and make me feel heady. Suddenly, I began to see the walls of the doorless passage close in on me from both sides rapidly and, in the end, form the shape of a coffin that would perfectly enclose me.

'Let me go,' I said, this time somewhat loudly, 'I will be back at the soonest, do not stop me.'

That's when my husband shoved me hard. As I hurriedly searched for the ends of a whole bunch of threads that had broken together in my mind, he pushed me from behind, again and again. I could finally stop when I caught hold of the bedroom door for balance. I saw my husband's face fleetingly, like a dying flame on a burnt-out wick. Maybe the expression that I saw on his face is what I will call murky fire. He rubbed his oily hand on his head, chest, and stomach and pushed me onto the bed. As I fell on it helplessly with my soured, seething pride, I saw it all. In a moment like this yesterday, I cried in a way that was beyond human. I became terribly afraid. My husband had closed the windows and bolted them so tight that not a drop of light would enter; he was now closing the door, the only exit. Maybe he was going to beat me. I must go out after that at least and walk a bit in the blazing sun. Again, fire, burning bright, came to my mind like an alluring thing. A fire that burnt like flowers blooming. My husband stood by the door, his hand on the lock, looking at me. On his neck, that big blob rolled each time he swallowed. When I rolled through the dark passage all alone, he must have stood like this, watching quietly, I thought. With that, everything seemed revealed to me. All those closed windows and doors. Still lying on the bed, I hissed like a python: 'Let me out. I can't breathe. I am tired.'

I think I was also struggling to breathe, actually. I felt unbearable irritation, hate, anger, and fatigue. I stood there and saw the walls of the bedroom turn to stone, and my husband dissolved into the darkness rising around me slowly, surely like water dripping from a tap. In that sadness that made me want to cry, I rushed towards the door like someone on a sinking boat leaping into the water with no other way out.

My mind was filled with anger and disappointment and terrible fear. 'Let me out,' I yelled. 'I'll kick this door open!'

In the swelling silence, my voice acquired the gravity of disembodied, divine sound. All alone in the silent dark, I was on this side of the door that barred my way like an awful monster. I was suddenly struck dumb with terror. I stood staring meaninglessly, eyes wide open, at that door. Maybe I am wrong there. There was no door at all. I was anxiously staring at the darkness. I felt I must fall at my husband's feet, beg him to show me where the door was and open it. Pride is always relative. Anyway, I would not open any door with this mind so worn and fatigued. The sound of my breath drove me mad, like the whistling of the wind sweeping through a parched and empty landscape. I thought about my husband, who stood in the back of my mind like a dead tree: a piece of iron, like the one I saw in my dream, would soon sink into his neck.

Like a wild beast trapped just then, I paced many times around the room, sniffing the four walls and growling. As my footsteps and breath rang in my ears and drowned every other sound, the small room suddenly began to grow long and narrow like a passage. That's when I started to run fast to see the end of that winding, long passage. As I rushed headlong into the pitch-black, I found a tiny pore of light as small as an ant's hole. Maybe because there was nothing to do but run, I began to scratch and dig at it like a desperate animal. Suddenly, little grains of light fell on me like fine sand. That's how I saw the Prince. He was richly adorned and sat high above astride on a winged horse with its wings spread out; he held a glittering sword. The grains of light that fell on me had emerged from his laughter.

Sitting on his gleaming saddle, the Prince held his hand to me as I stood below. I took his hand and climbed on the horse with him. He caressed my hand and asked, 'What is it that you want?'

'I want to fly,' I told him.

'Where to?' he asked.

I thought a lot about it. Where to fly? In the end, I told him, 'I am not sure where. Please tell me where.'

The Prince laughed again, scattering the tiny grains of light. Then he looked at the diamond-studded pendant on the chain around his neck and said, 'Make her a princess!'

At once, I turned into a stunningly beautiful princess sparkling with jewels from head to toe. The folds of my garments were the waves of the ocean. The gems in my hair were the stars sparkling high above.

'Now, I will give this princess a sword,' the Prince declared. 'But the sword you swing cannot return without meeting its target.'

The powerful sword and the crown gave me endless confidence. I travelled a long way in the sky with the Prince. When I was flying thus, I saw my husband below beside the locked door like a mere sentry.

'Lower me, please,' I requested the Prince. 'I'll be back soon.'

I descended quickly like a bird's feather falling to the earth. There, I touched the ground right before my husband with my sword and crown, my jewels and my greatly grown sense of myself. I had become very beautiful and a princess; he gaped at me for a few moments. Maybe because of the sneer of contempt that woke on my lips in response to the disbelief and discontent on his face. But in the flash of a second, he leapt at me with the agility of a hunting dog. He knocked down my golden crown in a fraction of a second. That was completely unexpected, I have to say. We fell on the floor of the room like a pair of dogs tearing each other apart. With that, my mind became like a tent, all the cords of which were cut. The darkness welled up and rushed through it like a river in spate. Seeing the golden sword lie orphaned amidst a thousand sundry things in the room, I felt insulted like a queen slapped by a mere enemy soldier. My Prince up there must be seeing my defeat and humiliation. The sallow, wan neck right in front of me. My eyes drilled into it. Then I remembered that I had to return to my Prince very

113

soon. I picked up my sword like a queen. I don't know what provoked me—the slimy neck that shone like the back of a venomous snake or the sword—to kill my husband. But all such details are irrelevant. When he collapsed on one side from where he stood, his arms now hanging loose, his face was not at all like what I had expected. Death makes us all worthless fools! The face of the man who collapsed at my feet was like that of a jester. I pulled a white mundu left to dry off the clothesline and covered his head. Because I did not feel drained, I smoothened our bed sheets which were all wrinkled and crumpled and replaced all the things in the room that were strewn around, making it neat and clean. Whatever it may be, there are some courtesies we have to pay to death. Death will come, of course, to even the prince and the princess. But even though I tried to finish it quickly, I think I was late. Outside, the Prince and the winged horse did not wait for me. It's my fault. I should not have descended to the earth trusting the swish of my powerful sword. I need to tell all of this to my Prince. That I am very scared of being alone and that I am going to fling the sword away. But I have to wait. That's why I am sitting on the steps of this veranda. After all, the fault is mine.

('Rajakumariyude Vaal', 1979)

# Bhanumathi's Morning

It was very late when Bhanumathi woke up. The alarm had not rung. The battery must have run out. The clock was still at 12:10 midnight.

Rohith had taken a long time to go to sleep last night. She did not know why—if it was a stomach ache or an earache. It was as though there were no other adults in the house; she had to soothe, caress, hold, and carry him so that he would feel better.

Raghunathan turned in his sleep once or twice as though he were irritated at the disruption. In any case, he was useless in such moments. And she would have to suffer, on top of it, the grand declaration that the child wasn't sleeping because the mother was no good as a caregiver. It was three in the morning when the child sobbed himself to sleep. Her body and mind were both exhausted. She didn't sense dawn arrive at all.

She opened the door; her heart almost stopped. The milk was not delivered. There wasn't a drop of milk in the house. She had to get to the office on time today. It was impossible to get there before eleven if she went out for the milk and cooked breakfast after.

Glancing at her watch once more, Bhanumathi ran to the kitchen. She had to wash the dishes and have a bath before Rohith woke up. Then he had to be given a bath. If she woke him up now, he was sure to throw a tantrum. The milk had still not come. But the ayah from the crèche would be here anytime now to pick him up.

'Raghu, the milk isn't here,' she said, shaking him awake. The Kamadhenu store had milk. Rohith will start bawling now. I have to be on time at work today. 'Uh,' grunted Raghu as he turned over, as usual, going back to sleep. She pulled off his blanket in a rage.

She said, 'Enough of sleeping! I have to get to the office on time today!'

'Did I say that you shouldn't? Uff, the nuisance!'

Bhanumathi squirmed with desperation as she stood there.

No words would make a difference. From the time they shifted to the city with the child, she had wished for a helping hand at home. Hearing the child's wails when she set off to work made the guilt boil inside her. But to stop working was simply not possible. They were both slaving but could hardly make ends meet. It was true that Raghunathan was an engineer. So what? The rent and milk and electricity bill were paid from her salary. Also, even if it wasn't so, can one just drop one's career abruptly?

Remembering that Raghunadhan would fuss if she didn't have breakfast ready, she opened the kitchen tap. 'God!' How cruel could the world be to a housewife! The half-bucket of water left was not enough even to brush her teeth. Bhanumathi lost her cool and kicked the bottom of the pipe a couple of times. She knew well that this Chaplinesque gesture did not look very womanly, but in such situations, emotions always take the lead. As if to demonstrate the disadvantage of it, the bucket capsized and was soon empty. Woken rudely by the sharp sound of the iron bucket falling, Rohith began to cry. 'The child,' called Raghu, 'Bhanu, can't you hear? Its throat is breaking!'

'Ah, let it! It won't hurt your arm to pick him up once!'

'He's soaked in piss and shit—fine mother you are! Look at it! Nobody would believe that its mother's alive!'

'I have to leave soon for the office today. Didn't I ask you to get the milk?'

'Is the child swimming in its own piss because I didn't get the milk? You have always been quick with retorts!'

How to wash the kid without a drop of water in the house, thought Bhanumathi. She would have to go down and get a bucket of water up here on the third floor.

The programme had to be actually submitted yesterday. The final touches still remained to be done. She had planned to get there early and work on it.

'Raghu, please, pick him up. Can't you hear the child cry?' Bhanumathi hissed as she picked up the bucket and went out to get some water. She couldn't go down for the milk again, and so tossing the purse into his t-shirt, she reminded him, 'Don't forget to get the milk!'

'Not enough to pull a long face—you need to know how to run a house,' Raghu yelled. 'The imbecile! No milk! No water! Not a moment in this house without complaining!'

'Yes, we aren't living in a palace, are we?'

'The Princess sounds like her old man had covered her in gold when she came here!'

It was nearly eight. She was not going to wriggle out of this hell today and get to work on time even though she stood on her head! This whole Sivapurana was simply because she had asked him to hold the child a bit! If only she had chanted her prayers instead, at least this tedium would have vanished! But Bhanumathi did not say another word. That would only worsen the delay.

You have just witnessed a morning in an average middle-class family in a city. Not that the intensity of womanliness in Bhanumathi had somehow dissipated; the thought of it was precisely what made her knock down the bucket earlier. Though all the water was lost, the truth was that she felt lighter within.

As she was going down with the bucket, Bhanumathi thought how wonderful it would be if she were granted the status of a husband. To be able to sleep to one's heart's content at least one morning, with arms and legs relaxed and flung about, mouth open. But to think this way was an oversimplification. And besides, to limit Bharatheeya Womanhood to access to a bucket of water and slack-jawed slumber would be a gross indiscretion.

Bhanumathi was not too fond of Madhavikkutty, the woman from the nearby building, who Raghu always referred to as 'that other female'. The flashing red on her face when she spoke irreverently of Seetha and Savithri—wasn't it a bit too much? she always felt. But when Madhavikkutty got on a scooter and sped off, her smile and saree billowing in the air, her mind did pause with intense longing. This blackened serpent here, this *karkkodakan* in her house, her husband that is—if she merely uttered the word 'scooter', his face would be swollen for a whole week as though stung by bees. Jerking his neck in that peculiar way, Raghu would ask, 'So you want to become like that other female?' (Just that neck-jerking ought to be a reason to demand a divorce, Bhanumathi often felt). In such moments, she felt that Madhavikkutty was right. Even if they call you a feminist, even if Raghu says that you aren't well-born, having a scooter was a great convenience, she thought.

Pushing the bucket under the tap on the ground floor, Bhanumathi stood stock-still with surprise for a few moments when it struck her—that if she had a scooter, good God, she would gain a full forty-five minutes before starting for office! She could drop Rohith at the crèche and save the ayah's wages! She could get a week's vegetables on her way back. Escape the scary queues at the bus stop. Be on time at the crèche and for the doctor's appointments. Avoid the babysitter's sullen face!

As she was mulling over all these possibilities and in fact, in a dream-like state, the bucket filled and the water began to overflow. A rage filled her when she noticed it. He must be waiting for her up there to make him his tea. If the child cries, if the milk isn't delivered, if late for the office—everything was Bhanumathi's fault. For a second Bhanumathi mused if she shouldn't leave the bucket there and go for a walk in the large maidan near the building. If she didn't turn up for some time, he'd somehow find

water, get ready, and go to work! But what would
he do about the child? She thought again. Would he
simply lock it inside and go to work in a fit of anger?
Maybe not. It was his child too, after all. More likely
that he would take it to Saradamma next door and
tell her, 'Bhanu's gone to the shop—will be back
soon—please take care of it till then,' and then go
off to work.

Bhanumathi shifted the bucket from under the tap
and thought again. She stood up straight. Like that
'other female' Madhavi often said, now and then, one
must stretch and stand straight and think about what
one must do. That's how Bhanu forgot the water.
Stepping away from the hustle and bustle of vehicles
on the road, she walked slowly into the bylane. The
cool wind on her face was pleasant; Bhanumathi felt
her mind grow lighter. This was new for her, like the
fresh feeling from wiping one's sweaty brow with a
wet cloth. She felt joyful. The computer and the child
looked distant, as though they were on a screen far
away. She decided to take a half day's leave and spend
time in the soft sunshine in the nearby park, sitting
quietly by herself. 'Forgive me, Saradamme,' she
inwardly whispered as she tucked the unruly strands
of her hair behind her ear, sitting and leaning on the
park bench. 'I have no other way. Am I not fond of my
own child?'

Her thoughts scattered suddenly to a warm afternoon when everyone was resting after lunch. Her aunt, smiling with Raghu's photo in her hand. 'Good looking!' Amma said. 'He is a good match for Bhanu.'

Caste and horoscope and wealth and good looks were all described and matched. Those were days when she believed that post-marriage days were all picnics and cinema and ice-cream times. It was her fault—she admitted to herself as she thought back.

In the dos and don'ts that Raghu had prepared for his wife, not just the Wimbledon finals, but even switching on the sports TV channel was forbidden. Since the Wimbledon finals always coincided with Raghu ettan's hour of hunger, like all good wives, Bhanumathi kept calm and maintained a smiling face. And 'Oh, that's a minor thing,' she added. And then, at the office, in Sharmila's cabin, watched a recording of the match on the small TV handset. So, office and work allowed her many things that the home would not. Born and raised by the sea, she loved to swim in the sea and enjoy the sea breeze on the beach. But Raghu did not like it at all. 'Oh, that's a minor thing,' she responded to this too. And then sat quiet, looking at the sea. Lata, who was her swimming companion, was on an official tour and would return only in a couple of days.

Otherwise, Bhanumathi remembered her wedding only on Sundays in that tiny one-room-and-kitchen flat when Raghu took over the room to watch TV and play cards, and Rohith's tantrums dashed on the walls of the limited, enclosed space of the kitchen. Many a time she felt that . . . all that people said about marriage, inside the family and outside, was a fraud. Her lack of insight back then would irritate her like an annoying strand of hair brushing her face. Why am I so scared to do what I wish? It was as though someone always yanked her back from behind. But there was no point blaming someone or something else for everything. She should have tried to get in advance a sense of what marriage entailed; she, too, was responsible.

Suddenly it struck her that her train of thought that day was unusual, and how long would she watch the Wimbledon matches like this in secret? Why do I withdraw each time? Surely, not out of affection for Raghu. I live with him only because ninety per cent of people think it is the common, normal thing to do. Rohith was not born out of undying love. That, too, was just the result of the fear of stepping out of the normal, the usual. The more she thought, the more contempt she felt for herself.

Because her mind had turned turbulent again, though she was sitting in the park, and though the day had fully dawned and the breeze had begun to blow, Bhanumathi's mind began to splutter like oil in a hot, wet pan. A sharp burning sensation spread through her mind, like hot drops of oil splattering on the skin. Rohith's face rose in one side of her mind, raw and painful like exposed flesh, and on the other side, Raghu's face full of derision for Madhavikkutty. This is why she left the park, leaving aside any thought of consequence. Good that I decided to get the milk myself and take the purse, she thought. She knew that she wasn't dressed properly. But she told herself, as Madhavikkutty would say, the dress is actually less important. She pulled her comb out of the purse, combed her hair and tied it up neatly. She went over to the public tap and washed her face and strode ahead. At least this time, I shouldn't retreat. Encountering great difficulty in focusing on that point without blinking, she tried repeating that sentence to herself again and again. That was one reason the shop manager was somewhat taken aback by Bhanumathi's enthusiasm when she hurriedly ran into the shop where she had seen the scooters displayed—a sight that had made her pause wistfully over and over on her way to work and back.

'You are alone? Just saw your husband pass . . .' he said.

'Ah!' she responded, 'Don't we all need the courage to take at least one decision by ourselves?'

'I have decided to get a scooter. That makes it easier to reach the office . . . Rohith is with Saradamma now.'

Now, feminists will demand that the story must end at the point where Raghu realizes that Bhanumathi, like Madhavikkutty, was now getting a scooter for herself, deciding for herself, and thereby becoming a feminist herself. Because one would expect in the normal course of things that Raghu would see his mistake and turn a new leaf to become a good husband. But life is always more complex than art, so Raghu refused to let Bhanumathi back into their home.

And taking into account the fact that she was his wife, he shoved her away and ordered her out. Only then did Bhanumathi realize that getting the scooter was merely the opening act of the play. And so, she stood there, not moving much, looking straight at him.

When he asked have you become so bold, she retorted, unusually for her, shouldn't I be at least this bold? It wasn't just that asking thus made her happy; her mind also became calm and clear like serene waters.

So, this is how you become a feminist? Bhanumathi asked herself, filled with wonder. So easy? When she stepped out to collect water that morning, she had no intention of becoming someone like 'that other female', nor did she think she could ever be. She had merely decided to get herself a scooter, and there her husband was calling her a feminist!

She felt tickled, like getting soaked in the first showers of the year. So, this was all to it . . . 'Oh, never mind, that's a small thing,' said Bhanumathi, maintaining the long time continuity in her conversation with Raghu. 'Anyway, what's the point of staying under a roof to quarrel all the time? I usually feed Rohith a banana when he wakes up. If you can, give him one.'

'So, you will leave him here? Are you a mother?'

'What if the mother goes away?' She laughed. 'He's with his father! Why, Raghu, will you love him less than me?'

After this, I can write anything—that she calmly walked away from that house or pushed Raghu aside and strode into the house full of confidence. Since both are the same, my reader, you may choose any yourself!

('Bhanumathiyude Prabhatam', 2000)

# Scars of an Age

Mrs D'Souza rubbed the cream briskly into her face and then washed it thoroughly with liquid soap. The remnants of the makeup flowed into the wash basin. The lips on which the red of the lipstick still lingered looked pale to her. She bit them hard. To look red, to look red enough, it took all of forty-five years.

She took another look at the mirror above the wash basin. Signs of age were creeping around. The cream now failed to hide the wrinkles forming slowly around the eyes.

True, they did not fade beneath the cream. At the office, however, she was still the 'evergreen'.

Many cast an envious eye when she wore pants and skirts that suited her slim body; she noticed that often. Each time, a fear flared up within. God, if I lose this . . .

Each day of work added a new minus sign. Not looking youthful is a disqualification here.

Youthful secretaries, youthful executives, youthful employees—youth everywhere, in the mighty pillar and trifling rust. The very sparkle of the office lay in its youthfulness.

Lips with no lipstick on them, hair with no dye, no colour, cheeks that did not glow—these are all outdated. And so, pose problems of survival.

The office login password is: 'Presentable'.

A word that made the fear drip all along the way—that's what Saraswathi, a little out of shape, said of it.

'I won't go in to give a leave application, even if I am unwell,' said Lina, not taking her eyes off the computer game. 'Alice is the one who takes it. You are forty-five but look twenty-eight. If that wasn't so, Gupta would have kicked you out like a ball!'

'The MD won't have the likes of me as even a peon!'

Jayashree leaning on her seat, her oily hair tied up, half a kilo of gold hanging from her neck, added, 'But I am not available to be on display in pants and skirts!'

'Oh, the grapes are terribly sour!' Lina's eyes were still fixed on the game.

Ramamoorthy, who had already received marching orders, stared at Lina. Come tomorrow, Gupta—the MD, that is—had ordered him. He then called in the finance director's secretary and completed the dictation.

(Even otherwise, it is Johny who decides whether my upper lip should be downy or not.)

Gupta is like that. I am helpless with some things, he used to say. Having an aversion to dark blue, his order to remove the painting in his room with too many strokes of dark blue came within half an hour of his taking charge.

She had felt greatly relieved. And very indebted to Gupta. Dark blue—she, too, detested it.

But the cashier, Sukumaran, adored it.

Many, who realized that dark blue to Gupta was like red to a bull, gave up the former. People in the office stopped using blue-ink pens, even. 'I can't help it,' said Gupta with a kind of helplessness. 'If there is even a touch of blue within my eyeshot, I can't think or focus!'

Gupta also had some undeviating ideas about how his personal staff should dress.

He liked people who dressed tastefully in light colours.

Sukumaran, who was generally careless about his dressing, opted for a different department three weeks after. 'I work with my head, not with what I wear!' he declared. 'If this is his way, I am going my way!'

Another obsession of Gupta's had to do with new footwear. If you told him, that you needed money to buy new shoes, he'd hand you his earnings. Lakshmi, who worked in finance, said, 'A screw's loose somewhere, surely. Why else would he be so bothered with what secretaries wear?'

It was a pleasure to see oneself climb the hurdles of career through uncompromising professionalism. That was a new experience in one's familiar work culture. The world of vigour and efficiency. The truth is that when she stood before Gupta, she never felt that she was a woman.

She mentioned Johny to him for the first time on an evening when they were relaxed and celebrating the successful execution of a particularly big order. To be precise, about Johny's restless, burning nature and the silence at home.

Gupta's gaze fell probingly on the bandaged wound on her arm from the sharp pieces of the broken mirror that Johny had smashed.

Even today, she did not know how she had found the courage to tell Gupta about it in the office cabin. She had been telling Lalitha about how she had dealt firmly with some young men who had followed her on the way home, passing obscene comments, and Johny had reacted to this . . .

Her mind was like an undammed river. In her mind, the image of Johny—freezing in shock with the food on his fork stuck in his mouth—stayed like a nightmare. 'And still, you won't admit, Amma, that all this is because of your show-off!'

Johny tugged hard at the phone wires and broke them. 'No, you won't admit it, Amma!'

'No,' she said. 'And if I was indeed showing off, that can't be used to justify the waywardness of another!'

I am not one of those who believe that if the husband dies, the wife should consign her life to the waste bin. It is another matter that Davies, then and now, was her beloved, her most precious.

But no one had the right to order her to accept him as her most precious. Not even Johny.

That was exactly what she had told Johny that day clearly.

'Amma, you . . .' he raged from where he stood, 'Amma, you . . .'

'I'll complete it,' she said, trying to fix the wires her son had broken. 'That you have the wherewithal to have me stay back at home, right? And that you are willing to . . . And why do I still strut around and show off?'

'Yes,' Johny agreed. 'What's wrong with that?'

'It is all wrong. Each one is responsible for their own life. Money and status and value as well as little dreams and desires—it is all part of this life.'

'You aren't just Alice to me. You are my Mother.'

'I am Johny's Mother, but also a full, complete Alice as well. It isn't right that Johny should expect his Mother's desires to be the same as Alice's.'

'Oh, things have gone that far, so!'

'If that is what is meant by I becoming myself, then let it be so.'

'You don't care what anyone else says, Amma! You may have no shame, but I do! I have to be able to show my face outside.'

'Tell me the truth. What is it that pains you? That someone said something lewd to Alice? Or to your Mother?'

'I will be enough to take care of my Mother,' he said. 'But about Alice . . .'

'Alice has to learn to look after herself. That's what I have to teach myself. You won't understand that, Johny!'

'Won't, won't, won't! Why is that?'

He struck the brass vase on the dining table. Its edge hit her arm, and it began to bleed. More than it, her mind.

That brass had pierced right through the layers of the sense of security she believed she enjoyed within the four halls of her own home. The layers were torn and scratched now, all over. No. Security inside the walls someone else had built was a myth like the rice in your neighbour's storehouse.

'It's all futile,' she said, leaving the brass vase on the floor, 'None of this is an answer to anything, Johny. This level is now over.'

Like a sweeping windstorm, a raging fire, he slammed the door on his way out.

'Great! Cheers!' said Gupta, smiling as he knocked together two glasses of water and handed one to her. 'To a people who take pride in Parasurama, who chopped off his mother's head in deference to his father's commands . . . to Mrs D'Souza's enlightenment!'

'You realize now that it is hard to shake off deep-rooted habits? Now drink up that water,'

She remembered Davies then. If she told him that someone in the office had made a pass at her, he would laugh and say, 'Ah, that just means that my Alice is a looker!'

When her voice showed the damp bitterness of irritation, he would grow firm as a rock.

'Just because there are thorns in the path, will anyone stop walking? If you turn back, you will be stuck behind where you started! Then don't look for me!'

Johny had nothing but contempt for her yearning to become a fashion designer and her passion for making flower baskets and wall décor from waste materials.

Gupta took all this up with much enthusiasm.

Work was a great relief. There was no need there to beg or plead with anyone. No need to convince anyone. A place where one could open one's wings with confidence. Nurse little desires that anyone would feel.

The wrinkled face began to become black like a burnt twig.

Mrs D'Souza stood there for another moment gazing at her face in the mirror.

Age lingered, smiling triumphantly on the lines of her neck.

High-necked blouses, workwear, may help to hide it somewhat.

Changing from her dress into a sari, as usual, she noticed that her stomach was beginning to sag. Her eyes wandered to it.

Her mind seared.

But Johny will never understand any of this. For him, fashionable dressing was a mere show, especially when it was his mother. Each day after work, she removed her makeup and changed into a sari only for his sake.

If that's what he wanted, let it be, she thought. It was so much easier than trying to convince him. When mutual communication seems impossible, much better to avoid scenes—you save time and energy that way.

Johny's tea cup crashed on the mirror and broke when she was looking at it, carefully removing the down from her upper lip. The mirror shattered.

'You're past forty-five! Who are you dressing up for?'

The muscles he'd developed working out hard in the gym every day bulged haughtily on his upper arms. He was standing behind her, hands placed firmly on his hips.

His arms were hairy. His voice bubbled with derision.

Her son had grown.

'For myself'—she didn't say that. She said nothing. She swept up the broken pieces, got inside the bathroom, and locked herself in.

The mirror in the bathroom was covered with mould. Not possible to use it to do the upper lip. Seeing her downy upper lip made the MD go crazy.

When he suddenly stopped the dictation yesterday, she was taken by surprise.

'A clean shave,' he said like it was a joke, 'for both men and women.'

'I think I've mentioned this multiple times,' he continued seriously. 'Facial hair . . . I can't stand it. Please do something about it, Mrs D'Souza?'

He did not continue the dictation though she covered her upper lip with her hand and apologized.

That day she had made danglers and lockets and bracelets from peppermints. 'That's getting you an increment for sure,' was Gupta's response.

When she came out of the bathroom, Johny was in the chair in the drawing room.

The door was bolted from the inside.

When she tried to open it without putting her office bag down on the floor, he grabbed her like an animal.

'Amma, you aren't going to the office. It isn't as if you'll go to heaven if you continue as Gupta's secretary! If you go, you won't have to return!'

His grip was tight and painful.

Mrs D'Souza felt her face redden like a burning coal.

'Who decides all this? You?'

'I, I, I . . .' Johny snarled, 'I, Johny D'Souza! Why? Have you any doubt?'

The Johny she had nursed and sung to sleep, of who she and Davies had dreamed. That he would be a different kind of adult. Johny D'Souza.

'Yes, Johny,' she said in as calm a voice as she could manage. 'This life and this house, both are mine. All decisions about these are also mine.'

'So, you won't listen to your son?'

'I'm not obliged to listen to your father, even. Move out of the way, Johny. You aren't even a thorn for me in the path your father laid out.'

The Mother who threw her son out, thought Mrs D'Souza when she called the police and her lawyer from the office. That's what they'll say.

Why should Johny leave home? The police, the office, the lawyer, the passers-by, and you yourself—will ask. A question that bears the scars of a whole age.

But between us lie scattered twisted brass, shattered mirrors. There stands bolted doors. And besides, the fatigue, the stink of failure, and opacity. Let me keep this life of mine for me to handle. That's a small wish. You should convince Johny of this. I—and even Davies, dead and gone—know that it is not easy. He might struggle, not able to see the trouble with staying protected. Johny may not be able to comprehend it if you tell him of the mind—which you are forced to own up from birth, which hunts you throughout your life, which separates the Alices from the Johnys and the Guptas, which sets our boundaries for us without us knowing. There are many who cannot . . . that is the sad thing. No matter how intensely you may wish, the scars that age leaves on your mind cannot be rubbed off that soon.

('Yugathinte Karakal', 2001)

# The Experiment

The needle pricked her finger when she suddenly flinched and drew back. She turned, letting the half-sewn blouse drop to the floor. The child had started again. Being naughty. Pulling away the saree's dropping end from its grubby hand, wiping off the blood from the fingertip, she asked. 'What do you want now, Renu?'

The child was angry. It stood there making whiny noises.

'So, you ran here because of this? Can't you go and play downstairs? It's not yet time for lunch!'

The child turned away. Now it tried to clamber onto the chair. Naughty! Soon, it's going to bring down all the books. She leapt up to steady the chair that was wobbling.

'I am sick of this! Get down right now, you're going to get a hiding, Renu! Where is Venu-ettan?'

When the child moved close to her and hung onto her saree, she picked it up and held it. She had lined its eyes with kohl in the morning; it had smudged her face.

'Why did you cry, *mole*, my dear?' she asked.

The child toyed with the chain that she wore around her neck and raised its eyes to her.

'You won't tell your auntie?'

Unexpectedly, the child sobbed.

'Did Venu-ettan beat you?'

'No . . .'

'Did he scold you?'

'No . . .'

'Then what happened, Renu?'

The child pressed its cheek on her shoulder and lay there quietly. When her gold bangles brushed against her chubby little thighs, she asked, 'Where are your knickers, mole?'

Lifting her short frock, the little girl said, 'In the garden.'

'Didn't Amma and Auntie tell you not to piss in the garden? You are a big girl now.'

'Venu-ettan took it off me.'

'Renu, what's all this on your thighs?'

The fingers of tiny hands pressed on the little-girl thighs made small depressions in the flesh.

'Venu-ettan pinched me . . .' The child's eyes welled.

Reddish moons from fingernails on the rosy thighs and shiny little belly. A flash of lightning passed menacingly in her.

When she picked up the child and went downstairs, the little one writhed on her shoulder. 'Don'wwant to play wi' Venu-ettan!'

She let the child down. Venu must be still under the mango tree. What a boy!

Devu was drying the firewood in the front yard. The sunrays fell on her red glass bangles and were shattered.

The wind had felled the children's toy temple, under the gooseberry tree.

In the banana patch—

Beads of sweat glistened on the firm, muscular arms and broad back. The length of the penknife tucked into the waist swung gently to the rhythm of the shovel rising and falling. Reddish down glinted on the ebony black of strong legs.

She leaned on the branch of the mango tree despite herself.

Suddenly, she noticed Renu's knickers lying in the reddish clay bricks in the garden. Venu was nowhere there. He must have run upstairs by now. As she was climbing up the stairs, she saw him. He was trying to stick the filmy red paper packing from an incense-stick box onto his eyes with spittle to peer at the sun. Renu had stopped crying; she was sucking the edge of her frock's ribbon and watching her brother's antics. She held the railings of the staircase. It is so easy to go down in this world!

Standing on a wooden stool, Venu removed the paper from his eyes and held it out to her. 'You don't want these specs? The sun is so pretty!'

Spitting the ribbon of her dress out, the little sister held her hand out for it. 'Can I look?'

'Will you cry again like that . . . without any reason?'

'No.'

'Never ever?'

'Never ever.'

'Then why did you cry?'

'It hhurtt . . .'

'How come, Renu? Auntie wasn't hurt?'

'Whe . . .?'

'When Velayudhan pinched her, she laughed. Loudly!'

'You're lying!'

'Yesterday noon, when I got on top to pluck the mangoes. It's the truth! Velayudhan pinched Auntie on her legs and chest and all over!'

'It's a lie! You were sleeping in Amma's room, Venu-etta.'

'I got off the bed softly when Amma fell asleep. To pluck the mangoes. Amma won't give us these specs if you ask her.'

'No, she won't . . . and then?'

'When I plucked the mangoes and threw them down, they ran, scared!'

The younger one pressed down her elbows and laughed.

'Also, Devu said that if you like it, you won't cry. Don't you like Venu-ettan, mole?'

('Pareekshanam', 1968)